# WE SINNERS

# WE SINNERS

## HANNA PYLVÄINEN

HENRY HOLT AND COMPANY

NEW YORK

Henry Holt and Company, LLC
*Publishers since 1866*
175 Fifth Avenue
New York, New York 10010
www.henryholt.com

Henry Holt® and 🄷® are registered trademarks of
Henry Holt and Company, LLC.

Library of Congress Cataloging-in-Publication Data

Pylväinen, Hanna.
    We sinners / Hanna Pylväinen.—1st ed.
        p.    cm.
    ISBN 978-0-8050-9533-3
    1. Religious fiction.    2. Middle West—Fiction.    3. Domestic
fiction.    I. Title.
    PS3616.Y55W4 2012
    813'.6—dc23

                                                    2011045670

Henry Holt books are available for special promotions and premiums.
For details contact: Director, Special Markets.

First Edition 2012

Designed by Meryl Sussman Levavi

Printed in the United States of America

1 3 5 7 9 10 8 6 4 2

*Then said Jesus, Father, forgive them; they know not what they do.*

*And they parted his raiment and cast lots.*

LUKE 23:34

FOR GUNNÀ

# Contents

# We Sinners

# FAMILY TREE

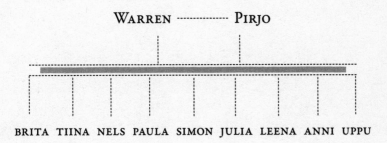

WARREN ·············· PIRJO

BRITA  TIINA  NELS  PAULA  SIMON  JULIA  LEENA  ANNI  UPPU

# POX

SHE SHOULD HAVE told him already about the church but she hadn't. The warnings were all there—he could name all of her siblings, and he looked at her too deliberately, and when he hugged her she was caught too long against his chest. Every morning she decided she would tell him, but every afternoon it was too tempting to go one more day, one more minute where he found a way to hold her fingers as she passed him a note. But now she knew he was going to ruin it all and ask her to the dance, she could feel it—she avoided him carefully but fussed with her hair, nearly sick with the twin terrors of him asking her or not asking her, not sure to which end she should assign her hope.

But he found her—he knew her schedule, and he found her lagging behind after class, talking to the teacher. In the hall he pushed at her shoulder with his shoulder and they seemed alone, despite the swarm of people.

"So," he said, "are you going to the dance?" She kept walking because it was a thing to do. "With me, I mean." She found this to be charming, and against her will she was flattered through and through. She looked at him. Her ears hurt with heat. She saw it was stupid to have ever pretended, even to herself, that she could go. "Well," she said, but the word caught.

"You're coming," he said.

Her smile was more mischievous than she felt.

"Please come," he said. He nearly whispered it in her ear. She looked at him. She detected sweat where his hair began to curl. It moved her, that someone like Jude could feel nervous talking to her.

"Well," she said. She thought of the many available lies— she had to babysit, the baby was sick. There was always something, there was nothing like six younger siblings for providing an excuse. But in her mind a minister warned that she should always confess her faith, and it occurred to her, Jude watching her, that confession was what it was. And she confessed. She said things about the church, her voice shaking out of time with her knee. She listed, idly, some things she couldn't do— nail polish and movies and music with a beat.

"So you can't go to a dance?" he said. "Someone's going to what? Punish you?"

"No, I mean—if you are tempted to do something, you know, maybe it's better to just not do it. So maybe there are good movies out there but I mean there are so many bad ones, so just don't watch them."

"Just don't dance, because dancing is—"

She blushed.

"Man." She saw on his face that she should not have told him.

"Sorry," she said softly. She wanted him to hold her, she wanted to sit in his big arms, like stupid girls did. She would cry. Hey, he would say, it's okay. Instead he walked away without waiting to see what she would do. She watched him go, watched him walk his easy lope.

Before her last class she thought she saw him down the hall, or maybe it was someone else, tall and heavy with dark hair. She pushed into the bathroom, where girls staggered themselves around the mirror. They put on mascara, only on their top lashes, two coats, one under, one over. "Hey," someone said, "is it true you can't even go to the movies?"

"Oh, that," Brita said. "Why?"

"Someone said."

"Oh," Brita said, "well, it's not that big of a deal." But she crept into a stall—she saw his name on the wall—and she thought about praying but it felt too vain to pray for something so small, and she didn't. She pretended to take a long time and she fished through her bag for nothing, but there was a line and she could hear the annoyance in the shuffle of feet.

She told Tiina what had happened. They were tuning their violins before orchestra. "Does everyone know?" Tiina said, a peg spinning free. "Do my friends know?" She nearly teared.

"Jeez," Brita said, "it's not that big of a deal," but she knew she was talking to herself. Still, she steeled herself, and she made it through the day, without seeing Jude again, without seeing his friends, without seeing her friends. She was almost out of the building when she heard their last name. "It's true," someone was saying, someone she didn't even know. "They're brainwashed. The whole family. They don't even have a TV."

Brita sat on the bus and pinched her thigh. She said the word to herself again and again, so it would mean less and less, and then nothing. The Rovaniemis were brainwashed. She was brainwashed. She thought about the people she thought were brainwashed, people who believed the world was ending on a specific date, people who saw aliens, people who believed meditating could make you lift off the ground. The Amish, with their claptrap horses and carts and orange reflectors to keep away motorized traffic. She felt better, thinking about people who were actually brainwashed, and she shook the word from herself, listening to the song piped through the bus, something she wasn't supposed to listen to, and she watched Tiina do her homework across the aisle, her pencil skidding across the worksheet, the answers easy and known. Tiina didn't look brainwashed—Tiina looked almost unremarkable, her hair softly brunette, to the shoulders, everything average except her eyes, hooded, heavy, hinting at Finns who had moved to America and married more Finns, and more Finns again. But otherwise she—they—looked normal, their jeans the same cut as everyone else's, only cheaper, their shirts bold and basic colors, rising to modest places, but normal. This isn't what brainwashed looks like, she told herself, and she took out her own reading.

When they got home, adding their backpacks to the pile at the door, her mother was abrasively cheerful, pinching everyone. "We found a house," her mom said. She did a jig. She said they were having pizza delivered. They never had pizza delivered.

"How many bedrooms?" Brita asked. She felt suspicious.

"Three, but, well, we can convert the basement into another. So four, maybe five."

Her mom took Tiina's hands and they jigged together.

"Four," Brita repeated. She went upstairs. She looked around the room she shared with her sisters, her dresser drawer askew again, her underwear hanging over the edge. She sat on the bottom bunk. She thought about the dance. She imagined what it was like to accidentally step on Jude Palmer's polished shoe, to smell his father's cologne in a darkened gym. Probably stupid, she decided, probably it was better she wasn't going anyway. It was okay, she was different. They were different.

They were in the world, but not of the world. And now they were moving, to someplace where people didn't know yet that they were different. She thought of her new teachers, their faces when they would meet her parents at conferences. Seven kids? Laughs politely stopped when they realized it wasn't a joke.

The school year mercifully ended. She did not see Jude, and he did not try to see her. She took all his notes and walked them out to the recycling bin at the end of the driveway late at night, stuffing them carefully between pages of newspaper. She said good-bye to her friends, pretending sadness but feeling relief, sensing already the inevitability of growing apart. Her friends would switch from one practice boyfriend to the next and fight for midnight curfews, and she would spend her Saturday nights at some church family's house, singing the same church hymns, eating cheese and crackers, always unable to get her volleyball serve over the net. She was seeing already that everyone was right, that believing friends were better, if only because you suffered together.

When true summer came, she threw herself into helping them move—of course her family hadn't hired a real estate agent, or movers, and they collected cardboard boxes from the dumpsters behind grocery stores. And of course in the midst of this, Julia—only five, but somber in her suffering—kept getting ear infections and needed tubes put in her ears, and their van broke down again, and again her dad would come home silent, bitter about needing to buy a new van at the same time they were trying to buy a house, snapping when no one brought their dishes to the sink. "You want me to put them away, huh, me?" he said through his teeth. Worse, their new home wouldn't be ready before they moved, and they needed somewhere to live for the intervening month. Instead of going to a motel, like normal people, her mom had decided they would move into her cousin's apartment since she was gone for the summer, trying to get engaged in Finland.

When they had finally packed a storage unit with cribs and bikes and bunk beds, everything in multiples, they drove out to their cousin's apartment complex, her parents quiet, a church CD on, the windows down. They piled out of the van, hauling sleeping bags and garbage bags stuffed with clothes. A woman in heavy makeup and dyed red hair was wagging her finger, trying to count them as they marched up the back stairs. "Seven," her mom said to the woman, sharply. "No divorces. No twins." Brita slung the baby on her hip, lightly.

In the apartment she stood in the living room, which was also the dining room, and looked around herself at the miniature stove, at the couch, which did not pull out into a bed. The confines of the room packed and amplified the heat. On the kitchen table there was a note from her cousin. Eat the food, it said. Avoid the landlord, white hair, big dog—he didn't know they were there. She missed them. Love and God's Peace— these final words in Finnish.

At night the heat did not rest. Brita put her pillowcase in the freezer, but the relief was so temporary it was hardly worth the wait. One month, Brita thought, but when she woke she discovered she itched. She touched her face, the back of her neck. She looked at her arms. She looked around herself, at the waking kids and her mother, in the kitchen making puuroa, as if anyone wanted to eat something hot in this weather. She looked at Tiina, who was trying to ignore the baby climbing on her back and pulling at her hair. She saw the spots on the baby first, then on Tiina. She checked the little kids. "Mom," she said, "Mom, come look," and when her mom began to laugh, Brita could not.

"It's the chicken pox saga," her mom said as they ate a lunch of bologna-and-cheese sandwiches on the living room floor, because now the folding table was covered in calamine lotion and the diapers, and newspapers with ads for new vans circled in crayon.

"Maybe we should get a hotel," her dad said. Her mom laughed and laughed. The little kids laughed because she was laughing. Her mouth was open and Brita could see her fillings.

A week of oatmeal baths passed. The little kids rotated in and out of the tub, and by the time it was Brita's turn the water was not even lukewarm, the residual oatmeal still on her feet when she stepped out, the towel damp from the other kids, the knob turning and jostling as someone tried to come in. All day she itched, but she would not scratch. She had a vision of appearing at her new school with scars, and every day she counted the number of pockmarks on her face. There was one particular mark that, in its close proximity to the somehow sexual organ of her mouth, she desperately needed to fade away. She borrowed winter gloves from her cousin's closet, so she couldn't scratch, but at night she would wake to find the gloves strewn and her scabs bleeding.

When it grew dark her parents let her and Tiina go outside. They sat on the back stairs and sniffed at the cigarette butts. "How do I look," Tiina said, posing with a stub hanging between her lips.

"Stupid," Brita said, but she thought Tiina looked cool.

"Do you miss him?"

Brita rolled her eyes.

Otherwise they never left the apartment. "I'm being held hostage," Tiina would scream from time to time, without prompting. She taped strips of paper to the windows to look like bars.

Her parents took them out a few times, to places with air-conditioning—outdoor-equipment stores, the mall—but people stared. They looked like the walking plague.

"Look, Mom," a little kid said, "it's the chicken pox family."

At last her parents left them home alone. "Kids in charge," her mother said. They said they needed to run out for more calamine, but really they probably needed a break. Brita and Tiina went into the bedroom and began to go through her cousin's dresser. They examined a collection of sporty thongs. They searched for love letters, makeup, and finally found a single stick of concealer.

The boys banged on the door. Julia had run out of the apartment, they yelled. Brita left Tiina with the little kids and made her way outside, along the balcony. She was nervous because she had seen the landlord just that morning, out in the courtyard with a graying dog. She hurried down the back stairs to the lower balcony, hissing in Finnish, rounding the corner to find Julia talking shyly to a youngish guy with a thick scar, wide as a finger, that cut across his brow. The scar ruined his good looks, making him approachable. "Dad ran over the cat," Julia was saying. "The other week, before we moved. He was so mad he broke the garage door." Julia wasn't contagious anymore—none of them were—but she looked contagious, with her picked skin and her tired eyes, and her starkly blond hair caught by sweat to her neck.

"How many of you are there, anyway? I keep hearing all these feet." He was holding plastic grocery bags full of frozen lasagnas and frozen pizzas and frozen french fries.

"Seven," Julia said, before Brita could stop her.

"Your parents must be pretty busy," he said. He laughed to himself. He shifted the bags from one hand to the other.

"What's your name?" Julia asked.

"Steve," he said, smiling patiently.

"Hi," Brita interrupted apologetically. She took Julia's sweaty hand, talking in Finnish, reciting the Lord's Prayer because it was the only Finnish she could speak in full sentences. She tossed her hair over her shoulder and did not look back.

Brita looked for Steve, but she never saw him. People went outside only to walk to their cars, or to let their dogs out, and so she watched the dogs play with each other in the courtyard like children, happy to be among their own. When the landlord appeared with his army buzz cut and giant hound, the others called their dogs in, leaving the landlord's dog to nose the doorsills alone.

Things were looking up, Brita thought. She hardly ever thought about Jude. The air was cooling. By the time evening fell, half the people in the complex were out on their balconies in folding chairs, sipping iced drinks. Her mom let them take turns sitting out on the balcony. The rest sat on the couch, reading books they had already read. In the kitchen her dad made roast beef sandwiches. The baby crawled into the kitchen and her dad pointed a finger at her and crouched down and said in a pretend growl, "Who's you, who's the chunkiest chunkerton I've ever seen? It's you, champer-damper, it's you," and scooped her up. It was the same voice he had used with the cat before the cat had died. He was good, people said, with animals and children, and when Brita saw him like this she wished he would still do that with her, but she was too old now to be teased, and too young to be talked to seriously. Sometimes he said things to her about work, or even money, but not in a confiding way. "What do you think I make?" he asked once, at a store, when she said she needed socks and then appeared at the register with new packs for everyone.

Above her father's singsong came the cry of a woman outside. There was a general launch to the door, except from her parents, who looked up tiredly from the lists of vehicle sales. "What is it?" her mom said. Out the window Brita saw the landlord making his way across the grass stiffly but steadily. She saw the red-haired woman with her hand over her mouth.

"Something with a dog," Tiina said from out on the balcony. Brita looked out the door—Steve was running along the balcony toward them.

"The landlord's dog bit your little girl," he said. Her mother rose sharply.

Brita stared at the sight of him at their door. She looked at their apartment, the sleeping bags everywhere. She bet the apartment smelled of them, of too many people. She saw him notice where cereal had been sprinkled and ground into the carpet.

Julia appeared with one hand over her back, the landlord behind her like an abashed parent. "She scared him pretty bad," he said. "She just came up behind him, and he's blind in one eye, he doesn't like that. Max never bit anyone before," he said. Julia turned around and Brita saw that Julia's T-shirt was stained with small pools of blood, like spilled juice, and her mom lifted the shirt to reveal a series of puncture wounds. More people appeared at the door, the red-haired lady with her little dog, the old Chinese man who smoked on the back stairs as if he were hiding it from his wife. They all stood at the entrance to the apartment and Brita tried to think of a way to get them outside and gone and not staring, but there was nothing to be done. The ambulance had to be called and a towel had to be pressed to Julia's back and everyone had to fawn over Julia and stare around the apartment.

"She didn't even tear up," the red-haired lady said, "not one drop. Steve saw the bite."

"Brutal," Steve confirmed. He eyed Julia's bite marks warily and made noises of sympathy. Brita couldn't stop herself from toying with her hair, but soon the ambulance came and took Julia and her mom away, and the apartment emptied—she thought Steve made eye contact with her before he left—and the landlord apologized halfheartedly, stiffly, clearly at a loss as to what to do about his dog, or this gigantic family camping out in one of his own apartments.

The landlord came by the next weekend to apologize again. "Anything I can do, let me know," he said. He spoke slowly, each syllable costing something. "Maybe this fan," he said, pointing to the noisy tumbling above them. Her mom said the drain was slowed from the oatmeal baths, and he knelt in their bathroom with no shirt on, jamming a plunger with surprising force. His body shook and he made noises that were awkward to hear, and he swore sometimes, and her mother pushed them away from the bathroom door.

Their neighbors sympathized with them. They told stories about Max nipping other kids, even his own granddaughter. Someone brought over cookies. Someone left a box of used markers and crayons at their door.

Brita wondered what Steve thought of them now, if he felt

bad for them. She shaved her legs with her cousin's razor and used her cousin's concealer stick on her pockmarks, and she borrowed the red-haired lady's folding chair and sat on the balcony with her feet up on the railing. She made ice water and wore sunglasses and imagined the sun was tanning instead of searing her.

She had chilled her legs twice with the melting ice cubes when Steve came out, walking through the courtyard, not toward his car but toward the landlord's door, at the corner of the complex. She watched him walk, hands in his pockets. He had a more hangdog air than Jude—more guarded, she decided. He knocked, stepped back, knocked again.

"Yes?" she heard the landlord say, not quite friendly. Brita sat up in her chair and leaned against the railing to watch. Steve had a broad back, a swimmer's shoulders.

"I was just coming," Steve said, "because—I'm on the lower floor." He said something else, and then she heard, "—the baby's always crying."

Brita burned. Everything burned, her face, her ears. She tried to get up slowly, but her sweaty skin stuck to the chair and the chair clanged against the cement. She moved to the edge of the wall and tried to pull the chair quietly shut.

"Are you okay?" she heard Steve say. Brita turned back and saw Steve leaning over the fallen form of the landlord. Max was keening, licking his face with perverse exuberance. "Hey," Steve said, looking up, noticing her, "you guys have a phone, right? Can you call and get help?"

She ran inside and got her mom to call and rushed back downstairs, the little kids following. She'd gotten as close to Steve as she dared, when she saw that the landlord had, all over his face and hands, the familiar scabs of their chicken pox, only heavier, not like a childhood sickness but like a disease. Along one cheek the pox was so thick she couldn't see the space of skin in between. Other neighbors showed up. The red-haired lady leaned over the landlord and put her hand to his forehead uselessly.

"What's going on? Is he okay?" her mom said, appearing on the lawn. She chatted anxiously with Steve. Brita saw that her feet were bare, like they always were in summer, and she wished her mom would wear shoes. She saw her mother suddenly as Steve must see her, her face pleasant and round like Finnish faces could be, but devoid of makeup, giving her a harried look, especially with her hair hanging limply in the heat, curling some from an old perm. She looked, Brita realized, tired. She looked her age—she looked like someone with too many kids, someone too busy to wear anything but a black cotton dress.

"We can take him," her mom said, pointing at Max.

"Are you sure?" Steve said. "Really, it's okay."

"Julia just scared him before—it'll be fine," she said. "And it's only fair," she added, with an ironic smile. Steve shrugged and handed her the leash. "Kids, come," she said, "up," and they went, Max slow going up the flight of stairs. From inside the apartment they stood and watched the ambulance arrive, with its lonely whine and beating lights. They watched the paramedics wheel the landlord away, and then Steve make his way back to his apartment.

Julia cried and said she thought Max was going to bite her again.

"You have to get back on the horse," her mom said firmly. "When I was little, I was maybe Brita's age, I fell off Big Red and he bit my arm, and even while my arm was bleeding my dad put me back on the horse." Tiina and Brita looked at each other and rolled their eyes. She always told this story.

Max roamed unhappily around the apartment. They put

out a bowl of water for him, but he wouldn't touch it. "No one try to pet him," her mom said. She kept the baby strapped into the car seat on the counter. The baby cried and Brita tried to amuse her by hanging things in front of her face, keys, measuring spoons, her hair, but she was too old for that now. Finally Brita lifted her and walked her around the apartment, trying not to think of Steve and what he had said about them, trying to keep the baby from crying.

Her dad came back from looking at vans. "No seat belts in the back bench," he said, sighing. He saw the dog. "Why do we have this?" he asked.

"The landlord has the chicken pox," Brita told him, "from us."

"From who?" he said, as if he hadn't heard.

Her mom made them clean. Brita was sure this was because she was worried someone would come to pick up the dog, and she wanted the place to seem neat. Brita wiped the counter and rolled up the sleeping bags. Tiina found the vacuum cleaner and went at the carpet. The little kids threw all the toys in a cardboard box and tried to stack the books but they kept falling, and they gave up.

But no one came. Finally they unrolled the sleeping bags and turned out the lights. Her dad put Max in the bathroom with a towel on the floor and a bowl of cut-up hot dogs from the fridge. For a few minutes Max whimpered, and then he was quiet.


All the next day no one came. No one called. All day Brita stayed inside. She did not want to see Steve. She did not want to think of Steve. She hated that she had gone so quickly from trying to not think about Jude to trying to not think about

Steve. The little kids held races around the balcony and she yelled at them to run more quietly.

"Nels is cheating," Simon whined. "He keeps pulling my shirt."

"Cheat more quietly," Brita said.

Her mom sent Brita down to try the landlord's door and Brita moved hurriedly, in case of Steve, but she didn't see him, or his car in the parking lot. She knocked hard, trying to peek through the plastic slats of curtains, but the apartment was dark and silent.

Her mom called the hospital, but they wouldn't put her through. "Can you put his family on?" she said, tense, annoyed. His family wasn't there, the nurse said.

The little kids crabbed and her mom snapped and yelled at them and then broke down, crying. Her dad came home and saw her crying and yelled, and the little kids ran into the bathroom to hide from him.

"Let's just leave," her mom said, her face and voice taut with tears.

"You think I want to be here?" her dad said. "You think I think this is fun?" he yelled, and then he turned around and left, and they all went quiet but he wasn't there to hear it. They all made their own sandwiches and poured their own milk and sat and read quietly, and the boys didn't even fight about wanting to read the same comic, and they spread it out on the floor and dripped jelly onto its pages together. They were in this tableau, the mood mild, almost serene, when her dad came in, carrying milk shakes and fries, cheerful as a form of penitence. "Serve it up," her mom sang, "nice and hot, maybe things aren't as bad as you thought." Fries fell to the floor and Max sniffed them but didn't eat them.

One more week, Brita thought, one more week.

*   *   *

The heat eased. By the end of the week it was only the midday hours that were unbearable, and in the shade of the balcony it was even enjoyable to be outside, but Brita kept inside. She napped and she sulked, and when someone asked her a question she gave the shortest possible answer. Often she simply sat and petted Max, but he hardly stirred. He didn't want his belly rubbed. She liked how he embodied her own depression. She thought she understood him, how he wanted to quit. If only, she thought, she could be like him and understand how little everything mattered. Everything bothered her. The little kids pinched each other and her dad eyed them moodily but said nothing. Tiina talked too loudly, all the time. Simon whined, about everything. Her T-shirts were all sweaty, so she took one of Tiina's and Tiina slapped her arm.

"Don't touch me," Brita said.

"Wash your own clothes," Tiina said.

"You're a little shit," she hissed at Tiina.

"Where did you hear that?" her mom said, dismayed.

"Dad," Brita said. The baby set off on a cry. She wailed, the rattle of a one-year-old, defiant, inconsolable. Brita picked her up and pressed her to her chest. "It's okay," she sang, "it's okay," but her tone was too angry.

Her dad sat at the table with his hand to his forehead. Nels picked up the recorder and began to play.

Her mom began to cry.

"Not you, too," her dad said.

"What?" her mom asked. "You think this is fun for me?"

"It's my fault," her dad said, yelling now, "that's right, it's all my fault. Blame it on me."

"Well," her mom said, "if you would let us stay at a hotel—"

"You think I don't want to be at a hotel? You think this is about being cheap?"

"No, I know," her mom said, suddenly contrite. "I know."

"Yeah, me, I'm a cheapskate."

"Dad," Tiina said, "Dad, stop."

"Warren," her mom said.

Suddenly he fell quiet. Brita turned and saw Steve at the door. He had a baseball cap on, highlighting his wholesome nature. His scar seemed laminated in the light from the living room.

"Hey," he said, "some people are trying to live here."

"Oh no," her mom said, "we're sorry, we're so sorry. The heat," she said.

"I know," he said. "It's okay, I get it."

"We're almost out of here," she said. "Two more days."

"Uh—did you need me to take the dog then, or what are you doing with him?"

"Well, we didn't want to bring him to a kennel while we were waiting, but we don't know what to do, he's not even eating." She was talking too fast.

"You didn't hear?" Steve said.

"Hear what?"

"Oh," he said. "Maybe I shouldn't say it, in front of the kids."

"What?" her mom said. "Is everything okay?" Brita felt something crawl around in her throat.

"Maybe there was already something wrong with him before," he said.

"Are you saying—"

There was a terrible pause. Steve lifted his cap and reset it on his head.

"Sorry," he said. "Yeah."

"How awful, how completely awful, I don't believe it."

"Yeah," he said.

"Is there—will there be a service for him?" She asked this somehow utterly calmly and politely. Brita looked around the room. The little girls seemed confused, but Simon was searching about himself, no doubt for the doll he was too old to be carrying around.

"I don't know anything about it," Steve said. "Sorry." When he walked away Brita stood at the door and watched him go. It felt like the end of the movies she wasn't supposed to have seen, the way he was walking off along the balcony, his body backlit by the balcony lights, and for a second she thought of Jude.

"Steve," Brita said. He stopped. "Sorry about"—she paused—"the noise."

"Yeah."

"Um, I'll keep the little kids quiet."

"Yeah, could you?"

"Yeah. And, you know, I know we seem crazy and everything but really—you know. We're not."

"Okay," he said.

"Really," she said, "we're not."

"Sure," he said, but she could tell he just wanted her to leave him alone.

She went inside and closed the door behind herself. She leaned against the door and fell to the floor. She knew she was being dramatic, but it seemed like the only possible way to be.

"What is it?" her mom said.

She smiled her mother's bitter smile.

"What?" her mom asked.

Her dad picked up a garbage bag and began filling it. "Let's go," he said, shaking his head.

"*Lähetään*," her mom agreed quietly. It took twelve garbage bags to fit everything, but they packed rapidly. They shoved sleeping bags under the van's seats, they threw toys and books and half-empty shampoo bottles anywhere they would go. They didn't clean the dishes, and they left the newspapers unfolded on the floor.

"What about the dog?" her mom asked as they did a final check of the apartment.

Her parents looked at each other for a long minute, then her mom took the leash and they walked Max out to the van. At the van door he brayed, and her dad picked him up and set him inside the van. He curled up in between the seats and did not stir.

When they finally pulled away, her dad rolled the van windows down. Brita stuck her fingers out in the air. Her mom put a tape on, and the bright, easy concerto suggested an easier world than the apartment they had left. Tiina and Paula had fallen asleep leaning against each other, their foreheads slick with sweat. Simon's head lay heavily against her shoulder, but Brita didn't move him.

"Where are we going?" she called out quietly.

"I wish I knew, Brita-boo," her dad said. She could not think of the last time he had called her that. He pulled them onto the highway. They drove for ten minutes, fifteen, and he stopped at a motel, parking beneath the overhang, but in a few minutes he came back outside, shaking his head. They stopped again, and again. Her parents dug through the glove box, through her mother's purse. They clawed for coins at the bottom of the cup holder.

"Forty-four," her mom whispered in Finnish.

They got back on the highway. They drove steadily, down roads Brita recognized but could not place. Her mom began to laugh.

"What?" her dad said. "It isn't funny." She fell silent, and when they finally pulled into the parking lot of the church her mom said, "Well, at least for once we'll be on time."

Her dad turned the van off, but the little kids kept sleeping. Brita watched her parents walk to the front of the church and unlock the door. She watched them haul in the sleeping bags. One by one they undid the seat belt of each kid, slipping the strap slowly from their limbs. One by one they carried each in. Max lifted his head each time but did not move.

When she was the last one left, she lay quite still. Usually her dad shook her, so she would wake and walk herself in, but this time he leaned in to lift her. As he carried her she felt him breathing hard and she knew she was too heavy. "It's okay," she said, as he struggled. She hobbled down to the ground.

She followed him into the church, up the linoleum steps to the sanctuary. Inside, the little kids were laid atop sleeping bags set out on pews. Brita found the last sleeping bag and lay down. She tried to adjust the end of it to build a pillow. She looked around the room. One of the windows was cracked and she saw the top of a tree, its branches burdened with leaves. At the front of the church, the cross was dark against the white concrete bricks—too small, she realized for the first time, for any man to hang upon its arms.

There was a stirring from the front of the church—her dad was pulling the front door, locking it. She heard the sound of Max's nails against the foyer floor, and then her dad lifting Max up the stairs. Max came into the sanctuary and found a spot between two pews and turned, three times.

Her dad crawled into his sleeping bag on the floor, all of his clothes still on. Her mother was already lying on her side on top of her own, the baby asleep against her. Brita realized her stomach looked bigger than she remembered, and she wondered if her mother was pregnant again. Probably, she decided.

"Pirjo," she heard her dad say as softly as he was able.

"Mm," her mom said. There was the distant tritone of a train. "Mm," her mother said again.

"Can I have my sins forgiven," he said at last. He spoke so quietly that Brita only heard the words because she knew what they were.

"Believe all of your sins and doubts forgiven in Jesus's name and precious blood," her mom said, tiredly but earnestly. "Can I too," she said, and her dad said the words back. There was the sound then of each of them turning. A rustle.

# HIS OWN HOUSE

THE SERMON STOPPED.

Warren's eyes wavered open. Up in the pulpit the minister's head was bowed, so that Warren could see his flushed scalp beneath the line of a comb. For a moment Warren could not place what was wrong, but then he realized that no babies were crying, no little kids were wandering in and out of the swinging doors. No one whispered. "Dear brothers and sisters in faith—" Howard said, and he pulled a handkerchief from his pocket but did not use it. Warren looked down. Lying on the floor, displaying her diaper, Uppu began to kick at the bottom of the pew, and Warren leaned over and fished for her leg.

"I have—" Howard tried again, "I have been speaking with some of our beloved brothers, and they feel, as I do, that this work of ministry has become too dear to me. I have enjoyed this work too much," he said. Warren glanced at Pirjo at the other end of the bench and she looked directly at him, her face impassive, which meant she was as shocked as he was. "I know that you will find someone more suited to this mission work, and I ask—dear brothers and sisters—could you forgive even this vanity?" Howard wiped at his cheeks.

After the closing song they mingled, Pirjo chatting and chatting, a storm of socializing, and the little kids raced between the pews, and the big girls loitered in the corners, avoiding adults. Warren stood aside, near Pirjo but not a part of her talking.

"Do you think John—?" Pirjo was saying.

"Well, for sure, or—maybe even Al Laho," Peggy said. "Maybe Warren," she said, seeing him standing there.

"Oh, not Warren," Pirjo said, laughing, "no, no." Warren managed a smile, as if Pirjo was being modest, when he knew she was being honest, and he rattled the change back and forth in his pocket.

Leena appeared, pulled at his suit jacket. "I didn't eat anything for breakfast," she said.

"Tell your mother," he said.

He went out to the van to wait. The kids followed, found books on the van floor, Simon reading and biting his nails. It was the end of fall and Warren turned the van on, to warm it.

"Someone run and get your mother," he said. No one moved.

Howard stopped by on the way to his car. He waved, and Warren rolled down the window and they shook hands. "You do know," Howard said, "your name may come up." There was the smell of coffee on his breath.

"Well," Warren said. He didn't want the kids to hear this. He cleared his throat.

"Well," Howard said, "it's all in God's hands now, isn't it."

Pirjo appeared at the van, Leena dragging at her hand. Howard leaned his large head through Warren's window to say hello to Pirjo, to say God's Peace to the kids. Be good to your parents, he said. Do your homework. It was the unbearable side of Howard, the constant admonitions, the way Howard thought it was his responsibility to drag your kid to you by the ear when he caught them listening to music in the parking lot.

The kids said good-bye awkwardly. They wanted him to leave too, Warren realized. Smart kids, Warren thought, good for them.

"Dad," Nels said when they'd pulled out of the parking lot, "are they going to make you a minister now?"

"No," he said.

"It's not up to us, honey," Pirjo said in her voice for the kids. "You see, the board gets together—"

"We all know it won't be me," Warren said. He felt the familiar flare in his chest. "Okay. We all know." He pushed against the back of the seat and Pirjo put her hand on his arm.


Warren's temper was mysterious even to himself. These things were supposed to run in cycles. "Was your dad like that?" Pirjo had asked once, after a shouting match with one of the boys. "No," he'd answered. "Then what's your excuse?" she'd said, exasperated, crying harder than the kids.

In fact, his father had been particularly gentle. He'd brought home penny candies from the shop, sat in the living room with the paper when Warren practiced piano. He'd had an unbearable amount of principle, true, making them swim at the cabin where his brother had drowned. And when Warren had moved south to the car companies, like everyone else, his dad had frowned. "I'm sorry to hear that," he'd said over the crackle of a poorly connecting phone. When the Heresy of '73 had come, they'd gone to opposite sides, his father and mother and six siblings to the more lenient Apostolics, but Warren—even then in love with Pirjo, whom he'd met that summer at a Finnish language camp—had followed Pirjo to the Laestadian side. "I'm sorry to hear that," his father had said, and again two years later, when Warren had become engaged to Pirjo. Warren had thought of this when his father died. He'd stood at the grave, his own first son in his arms. "I'm sorry to hear that." Not his father's last words to him, but they might as well have been. A polite way to express disappointment, a cruel way. Better to yell, to throw lamps, to punch holes in the wall—all things his father had never done.

Pirjo tried to come up with proactive solutions—counting to ten, walking away. "What does it," she asked, "what sets you off?"

Nels, he'd wanted to say, but he hesitated to say that. He was always slow to speak. He didn't like to say things unless he was sure they were true. And probably it wasn't Nels, not anymore, but that was when it had started. The big kids had been little and there had been the constant stink of pee that could not be masked by baking soda, and the sour smile on Nels's face when it was clear from the sag of his pants that he'd shit in his underwear again. And then he'd lie, say he hadn't, even in the van, when everyone could smell it. But now Nels was older, staunch, and stubborn. Now when he shook Nels, when he had his fist right by his face, when he held Nels up against a wall, Nels was only calm, steady, almost bored.

But it wasn't only Nels, it could not have been just the one difficult kid. It was daily things, it was money, it was when he stopped at the gas station and the kids all chanted, "Get a treat, get a treat," and when he came out with chips they grabbed for them like starving people. It was never having more than fifty bucks in the checking, the fear of having his credit card rejected, going to the zoo and having to buy two family memberships. Or maybe, more simply, just having nine children. But that was no excuse, he couldn't act like he'd just woken up one day stuck with raising two sons and seven daughters. He knew that.

Warren stayed up late that night, looking through all the church books from the shelf. The Bible, Luther's sermons, Laestadius's *Postillas*. In the front of someone's catechism he found what he was searching for, the exhortation to ministers from Timothy: "A bishop then must be blameless . . . not given to wine, no striker, not greedy of filthy lucre; but patient, not a brawler, not covetous, one that ruleth well his own house, having his children in subjection with all gravity; for if a man know not how to rule his own house, how shall he take care of the church of God?"

He brought the Bible to bed, opened it to Genesis, but he felt like a child, deciding to do every math problem in the book, even the ones that weren't assigned, knowing before he began that he would fail.

"It'll probably be John," Pirjo said coolly. She fell promptly asleep, looking oddly like their own children when her eyes were closed, her hair the same weak blond as the little kids', her foot twitching slightly. He wanted to kiss her shoulder, but he was afraid it would wake her and the gesture would seem calculated.

At work he couldn't think. Shyam was gone—he was getting married in India and couldn't move the date because it was fortuitous, according to astrologists, of all things, and then Shyam called that morning to have his vacation extended by two weeks. His boss had made it clear that Warren should have said no—it was only four, five days until quarterly taxes were due—but he could not seem to take the pressure seriously, and even staring at a spreadsheet that had been many days delayed he would be jolted suddenly by the possibility that the church board would ask him to be minister.

When he got home, Shyam's spreadsheets under his arms, the big girls were fighting, teaming up against Pirjo.

"It's just a phase we're going through," Brita was saying.

"I'm your mother—of course it's my business."

"Just relax, Mom," Tiina said. "We're just being teenagers." Down the hall, Uppu began to cry in her crib.

"Oh, good," Pirjo said, matching Tiina's snideness. "Warren, did you hear that? We've got another fifteen years of kids yelling at us."

"Out," Warren said, and he pointed with a finger. "Everyone out," he said, and he felt his jaw lock down. The girls left the room, sullenly. Pirjo put her hand on his pointing arm as she went to get the baby. He walked downstairs and he opened the door and he kicked the girls out. He locked the door. On the porch they sat quietly, like they always did. He stood and watched them, how their shoulders touched. Brita pointed to a spoon mislaid beneath a bush, and he followed her extended finger up and over the bush, over their unraked lawn and across to the neighbor's colonial, where plump garbage bags held the only evidence of leaves. Brita leaned forward and reached for the spoon. She wiped it with her thumb. He appreciated suddenly that his daughters, too, lived in a house where a spoon appeared beneath a bush, absent of owner or incident, no one knowing who was responsible, who to blame, and its very appearance so normal as to be unworthy of note. He felt suddenly tender toward them again, his daughters. He didn't know how to express these things, though, especially not to them. He didn't know how to hold them anymore. He didn't know what to say. How was he to apologize to them for having raised them in this kind of chaos? How did you say you were grateful— surprised, really—that they were bright and articulate and kind, when it had nothing to do with you? When he went back upstairs he wanted to say these things to Pirjo, to try them out on her, but she was in bed, snoring slightly, newspaper over her knees, coffee cooling.

As he fell asleep he thought briefly how strange it was to lead such separate lives—the work world, the home world— and how the one had nothing to do with the other. What do you do all day, Tiina had asked once. I figure out the difference between what things seem to cost and what things really cost, he had said, and for a second there'd been a visible path between the worlds, but it had closed just as quickly. Oh, she'd said, and turned away.

At work he thought about the same thing in reverse—what was it his colleagues thought of him, of his too-big family, did they think he was poor? He *was* poor, basically. Most likely, he decided, they only thought about how he didn't show up at the bar after work, or maybe they didn't think of him at all, the way he didn't think of them. Like Shyam, who had worked under him for nearly ten years, whose most distinguishing features were a self-deprecating humor and a nervous habit of running his tongue over his teeth, suddenly announcing he was having an arranged marriage.

"You've got Shyam's end under control, I assume," his boss had said to him in the break room. Maybe he had seen Warren's knee bobbing up and down.

"I will," Warren had said. He'd considered saying, It's not Shyam I'm anxious about. But it wasn't as if he would ever tell his boss his real worries. What faith was he? Probably Presbyterian—

probably some church with stately steeples where pastors wore white frocks.

On Friday he came home, the week supposed to be over but not over. He was late, he'd missed dinner—the bottom of the pot had been literally scraped—and inside he was reminded again of how Pirjo wanted him to put in the wood floors already. The paint was peeling off the plywood. But setting his briefcase next to the stash of backpacks, he could hear bickering from upstairs, the big girls fighting again, and he walked up slowly. He stood at the door to the girls' room. Tiina had been wearing Brita's jeans, it seemed, and stretching them out.

"They were sixty bucks," Brita said, "and now they're ruined."

"Honey, you didn't," Pirjo said. "Sixty? Really?" Everyone was somehow in the bedroom, no one wanting to miss out on anything, even a fight. On the floor Uppu played with a necklace, put it in her mouth.

"Just give her back her jeans," Warren said.

"Dude, just give them back," Nels said, playing the placater.

"I never get anything," Tiina said. "Brita gets everything." Her voice rose higher—"It's true, I never get anything." This maddened him because it was not true; it was payday and already the money was gone. She was being hysterical, it was a kind of show—ramping it up for the little kids, making her petty grievances into something momentous.

"For shame," Pirjo said. "How old are you?"

"Stop shaming me," Tiina screamed, and she picked up the nearest pair of jeans and threw them at Pirjo, the jeans falling clumsily through the air—they were not very aerodynamic—and one of the legs hit Pirjo in the face. From the floor Uppu began to scream.

"Is that what you want?" Warren said. "That's what you

want, you want to hit your mother?" And he reached for Pirjo, he dragged her farther into the bedroom—which was disgusting in that teenage way, the floor strewn with clothing, and books, and plates with dried bits of egg, and empty glasses of pop, and vanilla deodorant, and everywhere the stench of a sweet berry body spray, the bunk beds he'd built scratched and the sides sagging—and he held Pirjo, the flab of her upper arms in his hands, he squeezed her arms too tight. "Go on," he said to Tiina, through a mouth so tense the words could hardly come out, "go on, hit her, I'll hold her, is that what you want, you want to hit her? I've got her, just take a swing." Pirjo tried to pull away, but he hung on.

"Dad," Nels said, "stop it."

"I'm calling Howard," Tiina cried hoarsely. "I'm calling the whole church board and I'm telling them you abuse us."

"I never hit you," he said.

"But you would," she said, "but you want to," and he turned, he wrested the screen from the window, and one by one he chucked anything within reach out into the night, into the bushes outside—books and shoes, posters, CDs (probably pop, probably rock), a sewing kit. He chucked a painting of a kneeling girl—"Dad, that's mine," Julia screamed—but it was too late, and it fell, like everything else, and they all listened to its fall, a hurry through the bushes, a stiff crack on the concrete of the porch.


When he woke the next morning, their bedroom was warm and quiet with bodies. Pirjo was snoring lightly, and Leena's leg was wrapped about Uppu's stomach, and Uppu's arm was about Leena's waist. There was the smell of them, of scalps, of unwashed hair. He could see, clearly, the dark and hardened bottoms of their feet.

He made himself shower and shave and dress and head downstairs. He didn't want to see the wreckage but he knew he had to pick it up, before the neighbors saw. At the bottom of the stairs, though, he saw the big girls, Brita and Tiina and Paula. They were in their pajamas, big baggy shirts and soft shorts. Their feet were bare, their hair in tousles of ponytails. They were filling plastic grocery bags with books, not saying anything, their backs hunched, like they were picking strawberries.

He opened the door and stepped onto the cold concrete of the porch. He looked at the mess. Mostly everything had technically survived. The books were splayed awkwardly, pages loosened and bent, but you could still read them. The boom box was definitively dead. Julia's painting was bent—he remembered now that she had made it in art class, the teacher saying at conferences, like the teachers always did, what talented children you have, how do you do it. The clothes all finely fallen over everything.

A minute passed in which they knew he was watching them. He couldn't think of what to say. "Go eat some breakfast," he said at last. "Please." It came out scratchy. Paula and Brita stopped and looked at each other, but Tiina pushed past him toward the door, carrying her bag. The books were too heavy for the plastic and the bag was threatening to tear open. He reached an arm out toward her and she backed away sharply. "I got it," he said, accidentally angrily, but she just walked past him, and he heard her feet stamping up the stairs.

By evening he was forgiven, but he didn't feel forgiven. They had held a family meeting in the afternoon; like always, Nels picked the opening song and like always, he wanted to sing the closing hymn about night shadows, because it was only one verse long. They had all talked about the fight. He'd apologized. He'd cried, his heavy shoulders shaking, no noise, thumbs in the corner of his eyes. Everyone forgave him, and the girls asked for forgiveness too, slowly, deliberately, one by one. "Awkward moment," Nels said when it was over. The little kids tried not to laugh, and Warren wished Nels wouldn't joke like that. Then they talked about who was doing what chores, and who needed a violin bow, who had a recital coming up, and how from now on they would all do the chore assigned to them, and practice for lessons, at least fifteen minutes a day, each instrument—it's just a little bit of time, Pirjo said, and after all the lessons cost so much.

But even though he had cried, even though they had said the words, he didn't feel how he used to feel. He didn't have that wash of ease, the feeling of a bill entirely paid off, every finite and immediate worry put in its ultimate, insignificant perspective. He knew that forgiveness wasn't supposed to be about emotion, about how you felt—the absolution was no less real—but he remembered when the kids were little, when they lived in the small house and there were just seven of them and they all slept in the same bedroom. Brita and Paula had slept in the same small twin, because they both peed the bed, and almost right away he'd woken Simon in the crib. But he'd gone, on his knees, from bed to bed. He remembered the stiff cotton of Tiina's T-shirt. Will you forgive me, he had asked, will you forgive even me.

Remembering this, he got out of bed. He opened their bedroom door. "Brita?" he said now, into the room. "Tiina? Paula?" A little louder, he tried, "Julia?" He wondered if they were awake but pretending not to hear him. He moved farther into the room. Paula was closest to him, on the bottom bunk, and she slept like a doll, as if there were no difference between waking and sleeping but the closing of eyelids. Paula, he thought, what grade is she in? Sixth, because she had cried about needing new clothes for middle school, about not wanting to wear Tiina's hand-me-downs. That was the last time he had really thought about her so particularly. It was funny how kids were like that, how they drew different amounts of your attention. You cared for them equally, but you didn't show the care equally. You couldn't—you only moved your attention from one crisis to the next.

He walked out of the room slowly, so the floor didn't creak. He turned the doorknob steadily into place. In the hallway he stopped, stood. He prayed, silently.

May the Lord bless you and keep you. May the Lord make His face shine upon you and be gracious unto you. May the Lord lift up His countenance upon you, and give you peace.

He went to bed.

Like every Sunday they were late to church, but when they walked in someone had brought a tape player and placed it atop the pulpit. He found he couldn't listen to the disembodied voice preaching from the front. The microphone, he noticed only now, was laid beside the speaker of the tape player, and this only added to the surreal nature of the service.

The kids behaved worse than usual, maybe because the eye of Howard was not upon them, and twice Pirjo had to carry Uppu out. Once Warren turned around, as if to look at the clock in the back, but really to look at people's faces, to see if they knew something he didn't know. It didn't matter, he told himself—he could not be picked. If God was doing the picking, he realized, he was safe, for this room, this congregation, these hundred, hundred and fifty people—they might not know about him, but God did.

The sermon ended. There were announcements. The new-lywed who read them aloud seemed nervous. He held the papers in his hands, read haltingly. Bible class, Sunday school, the kitchen committee would be meeting at Peggy Maki's to chop the carrots and potatoes for the pasty sale. He paused. The board would be holding a special meeting on Tuesday to dis-cuss the new minister. Warren Rovaniemi was asked not to attend.

Warren did not turn his head, but he tried to look at Pirjo. She stared straight ahead. After the hymn, everyone seemed to disappear from the pew. Pirjo chatted almost ferociously, almost hysterically, about anything but the board meeting. The kids had vanished, like animals who could sense earth-quakes and smell storms in the penultimate minutes. He kept his hands in his pockets, looking to fiddle with some change, but his pockets were bare.


On Wednesday at work he had a package. It was the size of a child's shoe box and its stamps were not flags or hearts or famous people perched against a white background, but instead the stamps were stained red and pink, flushed with color. There was a card from Shyam: To the World's Best Boss. When he opened the package there were many layers of bubble wrap, and when he finally removed them all he was left with was a small figurine, the size of his palm. It was a god of some kind, with many arms, each arm extending out from the torso like a windmill. Each hand was cupped slightly, as if preparing to hold something.

He brought the god back to his desk and set it on top of the printouts of a presentation. All morning he felt like the statue was studying him. The phone rang and he jumped slightly, afraid it was Howard calling to say he must serve, he must be minister, but each time it was an ordinary thing—Pirjo, wanting to know if he could stop for milk; his boss, wanting to know if he'd heard how those fuckers on the third floor had screwed up this time—and each time the statue stared steadily on. Its placidity unnerved him slightly, its arms impossibly and evenly distributed.

At home he set the statue on the kitchen windowsill.

"Look at this," he said.

"In a minute," Pirjo said. She dropped potatoes into an empty pot.

"Cool, Vishnu," Tiina said promptly. How did she know these things? How is it, he wondered, that his kids were always ahead of him?

The little girls wanted to hold the statue. They whined, arms up toward the sill. "It's not a toy," he said.

The phone rang. The sound was coming from the living room, or from the foyer. No one moved to answer it. He walked to get the phone, but he couldn't find it, it was buried somewhere, under the cushions, or under the couch, or under the pile of newspapers. The ringing stopped, and he gave up. When he came back into the kitchen Tiina was holding the god, studying it carefully. He ground his jaw so tight it felt as if his teeth would actually cave in against each other. "You didn't hear me?" he said. He picked up a piece of mail from the counter—a bill from the violin shop, all those rentals they never paid—and pretended to look at it, to give himself something to do.

"You didn't hear me?" he said again, through gritted teeth. He felt something in his mouth crumble. He felt with his fingers—his crown had broken. On his fingers were bits of gold and dirtied tooth, and he bellowed out, mute, crude, like a beast with no gift of speech.

# KEEPERS

H ER PLAN HAD been to clean in the middle of the night, so her mother would wake to an empty kitchen sink, but as she stood in the foyer, the bathroom fan beating loudly and uselessly, the mess before her made her want to cry; being in a family of eleven made her want to cry, the way someone had soaked up the dog's pee but not thrown away the paper towel, the way that responsibility divided by eleven meant no one was really responsible.

Carefully, she threw away the peed-on paper towel, the banana browning in a lunch bag. She stacked backpacks, she sorted shoes in the shoe bin, and she was sweeping up a mound of dirt when she heard a car door close, and turned to see Tiina walking toward the house. She looked at the clock—it was a quarter to five in the morning. Tiina opened the door and stared at Leena, at the pile of dirt. She brushed the snow off her shoulders, off her hair, then headed up to their room, leaving a watery trail.

When Leena heard her mom's feet in the hallway she hadn't finished the kitchen. Her mom appeared in her panty hose and a blouse and watched her scrape a film of jam from the counter. "It looks like an elf came last night," her mom said brightly, pinching her butt. "Go wake the big girls, will you please, chunk, lovey," she said, heading to the bathroom to blow-dry her hair. Leena went up to her room. The big girls lay immovable in their beds. Tiina's clothes were piled on the floor. When she pushed at Tiina's shoulder she rolled over, naked, and Leena tried not to stare at the slump of her breasts.

"Shit," Tiina said, opening her eyes angrily, "everything is just shit today."

On the highway her mom passed back a hairbrush, and Tiina pulled at her hair, flicking water from her shower. "How come I'm not blond like everyone else," she said. "How come I'm fat?" Her mom snapped that it was a sin to talk that way. All of her children were beautiful. "What's that?" her father said. He was almost deaf in his right ear. Tiina had said it was because when he was in the Heresy he listened to music, but Simon had said that was stupid, no one ever went deaf that way, but either way, it was impossible for Leena to imagine her father nodding his head in time to a beat.

Leena looked out the window, at people in smaller vans heading to larger churches, churches with steeples and stained-glass windows, where people rose and knelt and dipped their fingers into bowls of water. She watched her mother reach out and smooth one of her father's carefully trimmed curls. He reached his hand out and she took it and the rest of the ride they held hands, straight into the church parking lot, her father spinning the wheel with the palm of his left hand.

At church the organist was late, and they asked Tiina to play. Leena watched her walk to the bench, searching for signs of hesitation, signs of guilt about where she'd been last night, but Tiina's face was smooth, and when she played her toes slipped confidently over the pedals. During the last verse her dad rose and Leena heard his bad knee cracking up the aisle. Her dad cleared his throat. "In the name of the Father—and of the Son, and of the—Holy Ghost," he said. Leena folded her hands, right thumb over left, the same way her dad did, which he had said once was less common, a sign that Leena must like order in the world, which was probably true.

In the middle of the sermon Tiina unfolded a note, not meaning for Leena to read it, but Leena saw it: Did he really call your thing a pussy? The word *pussy* was underlined, like something proud and important. Tiina folded the note back up, quickly.

Leena felt herself flush, just reading it. How did Tiina do it? How did she just sit there? she wondered. She studied Tiina's nails, looking for flecks of polish, but she didn't see any.

Stop doing this to Mom and Dad, she wanted to say to Tiina, they can't take it. Tiina didn't see how Mom had cried when she had run off with the car, she didn't see how Dad sat on the couch with the Bible, late into the night, waiting for her to come home. Tiina didn't pay the price of her own antics— the little kids did. Sometimes her mom said Tiina would grow out of it—Leena didn't know if this was really true. But Tiina's heart could be softened, Leena knew; once she had been taking a sauna, and she had heard her dad come downstairs and start ironing his shirt, and a few minutes later Tiina had followed. The way her dad had built the sauna in the basement she could hear everything through the vent, and Leena had stopped pouring water on the rocks, just listening. They were talking softly, but Leena knew—the whole house knew—that her dad had forbidden Tiina to go hear the famous violinist play the Sibelius. Do you know, Tiina had screamed, I am the only violinist in the country who is being forbidden to hear the very piece they are working on? And she had threatened to throw her violin, but of course she never would—she loved it too much. For several minutes there was only the sound of the iron, its hard hiss, its soft song. Then Tiina had begun to cry, and there was the sound of her leaning or crumpling against the washer, and her dad must have set the iron down and walked over to her. He forgave her. He said he loved her. I love you, he had said, and Leena had let the words be for her, too—she knew how hard it was for him to say these things. I love you too, Dad, she had thought, from the bench. I love you, Tiina.

Really it was almost a relief to hear him speak in his sermons. She could not recall a single conversation with him that was as long as one of his sermons, and so when he spoke she listened intently, as if trying to memorize what he sounded like when he talked at length. But he was always so serious in his sermons, always deep in the recesses of some troubled emotion. What was it like, she wondered, to minister to your own children? What did they look like to him from up there? Did he know things, had he heard Tiina sneaking out? Did he try to say the things that would reach her? He tried so hard. Once she had watched him icing the backyard, so they could skate. For night upon night he had stood out with the hose in his big Coleman boots, just thickening and thickening the ice. Why is Dad like that? she had asked her mom. Aren't you glad I married him? was all her mother had said.

"Sometimes our trials are personal ones," her father was saying. "I know for myself," he said, "I never see my sister anymore, who, as many of you know, long ago chose the world over the flock of the believers." Leena was listening now, and she could tell everyone was, even Tiina—her parents never spoke about their pasts, or even about their families.

"Even when I . . . called my father," he went on, "to tell him I had repented, that I had received this most precious gift of faith—that was the last conversation we had for some years." He looked down at his hands and for a few tense moments did not look up or speak. Then he said that sometimes he missed his family, that only a few days ago he had called his sister, and he had spoken to her about the Word, and how he could forgive her for even that great sin of unbelief. But she didn't want to hear it. That's how unbelievers are, he said. The Word makes them so uncomfortable, they can't stand to hear it. That's its power, he said, so great is its power.

Somewhere in the back of the congregation someone lifted their hand. "Believe all of your sins forgiven in Jesus's name and precious blood," her dad said, and then a few more hands went up and he had to say it again, and again, "Believe all of your sins forgiven, all sins forgiven," the words becoming more and more mumbled, more and more important, and she saw how he looked at each person, raised his hand up toward each hand. She felt struck suddenly by the need for him to see her, to see his own children, to forgive her, or maybe them, and for the first time in her life Leena raised her hand—she saw his surprise— but he said the words to her like anyone else, and her face grew hot with the attention, and she crept her hand back down. She half wanted to turn and say something to Tiina, to see if the proximity of the absolution had made her feel something, but Tiina only took a gum wrapper and folded it into a tiny hat, and a still smaller boat. Even during Communion, when her dad read the liturgy, Tiina looked bored. "Verily, verily, I say unto you," her dad read, ". . . and together with the thief on the cross"—Leena loved that, and together with the thief. Most of all Leena loved "Whatsoever thou shalt bind on earth shall be bound in heaven: and whatsoever thou shalt loose on earth shall be loosed in heaven"—sins being loosed and let go and gone, all of them keepers and loosers of one another's sins. But Tiina chewed another piece of gum, folded another boat.

When Communion started Leena watched her mother kneel at the altar, the back of her shoes thin and dirty. She watched her dad as he held out the wafer. The big girls and Nels rose to get in line for Communion, and at first Leena was relieved that Tiina would at least have to face that, that hypocrisy, but then Tiina turned and walked back up the aisle and out the sanctuary door. Brita and Nels just looked at each other, but their mom was bowing her head, and their dad was raising the plate of wafers, and the little kids were kicking at one another, and finally Brita and Nels went up to the altar without her.

Leena looked around. She got up and walked slowly, as if nothing important was happening, and she went down to the basement, where she checked the bathroom, but there were only the two Waaraniemi girls playing with the faucets. In the nursing room, there were four mothers with cloths over their shoulders. She wound up at the back steps and opened the door as quietly as she could, wondering if her dad could hear the door's tired squeal from where he stood, feeding her siblings the wafers.

Outside the snow was damp on her arms, and the churchyard looked empty. The bush out front, which made small berries that they popped in spring, had only thorns left, and though each spot in the parking lot was full there was no one around, like a graveyard, the cars markers of people but not the actual people. She walked to their van and opened the door—it was where she would go, the only private place—and looking in she saw the tip of one of Tiina's shoes hanging off the backseat. She got in and shut the door.

"Get out," Tiina said. "Please." She was talking into the seat, and her voice was muffled.

Leena dug below the bench and pulled out a sleeping bag. It smelled a little bit like pee, but she threw it over Tiina.

"Little Leena," Tiina said at last, "you are too sweet."

"No," she said. She thought about telling Tiina about all the books she had stolen from the school library. How when she cleaned the house she kept all the change, all the loose bills, how when they were at the grocery store she felt like dancing to the music. She had hated kids at school, kids who asked if they had electricity, who said they were Amish. She had envied all of her sisters, especially Julia, the family beauty, but even Tiina she had envied, with her confidence, and Brita too, Brita's capability with everything, cooking and cleaning and getting good grades and never complaining.

"You want to know something?" Tiina said. Tiina sat up and swung her leg over the bench. She climbed next to Leena. She pulled the sleeping bag over their chests. She considered Leena carefully. "Okay," Tiina said, "he's not from church."

"Oh."

"He's cute," Tiina said. "I promise."

"An unbeliever," Leena said.

"Well, yeah," Tiina said, and she smiled, like Leena had pointed out something new and wonderful. "Don't worry, okay," she said.

"Are you going to ask—" Leena said.

Tiina took her hand and Leena had the sensation of being

very small and, on the beach, their mother calling, Take your buddy's hand, everyone take your buddy's hand, don't lose your buddy.

Minutes passed, and the snow thickened.

"I'm cold," Leena said. As if bidden, the front door of the church opened and their father appeared. He wasn't wearing a coat. His tie wavered with the falling snow, and he was looking their way.

"Quick," Tiina said. She threw herself to the floor of the van, pulled the sleeping bag over her. "Come on," she said. Leena lay flat on the bench. They heard the sound of footsteps approaching, the sound of the van door opening.

"Are you actually hiding?" her dad said. "Get up, get out of there. It's freezing, get inside." He began to walk away.

Still on the floor, Tiina curled her legs into her chest. "Just go," she said.

"Just come," Leena said, from the bench.

But neither of them moved. The van door stayed open, and the snow fell, and the wind blew falling snow into the van, and onto Tiina's hair. For many seconds the snow did not melt. Leena was so cold she rubbed her legs together, but still she did not leave, wanting only to be kind, and feeling that waiting was the only kindness left.

# EYES OF MAN

PIRJO KNEW SHE wasn't supposed to buy a television. Believers did not use televisions. But she walked into the electronics warehouse anyway, her two teenage sons with her to deal with the salesmen who would look down on her, who would not realize she was trying to look down on them. At least Simon and Nels seemed to know about these technology things, each tall and thinned now, though Simon the taller and the more sarcastic of the two, with his perpetual boredom that she found so disturbingly effective. "This way, Mom," Simon said, and he walked efficiently, and she followed, trying not to feel the music—those thick insistent beats always scared her, the way they made her feel more alive—and when they reached the hundred TVs, a hundred screens displaying a hundred men pulling at a hundred lapels, she turned her head away before the boys saw her looking, hurrying to where the TVs were smallest and squattest.

Of course Warren had made it very plain that he did not want a TV. Learn math like the rest of us, he'd said, eyes closed, hands atop his hill of stomach, looking oddly wider than the kitchen bench he always napped on. But Donna Keranen had given her the math videos already anyway, and she knew she could fly through them, and in a month she could take her certification exam, and she would teach again; and besides it was absurd, it was really not that big a deal, a small TV, what could it do. They could watch that Lewis and Clark video the neighbors had stuck in with the giveaway bag of clothes.

"Mom, just pick one already," Simon said. The two boys stood staring at the TVs, their blond heads eerily similar from behind, but Nels's hair short and serious, Simon's hair long and flopping. Nels leaned in to examine the details on a TV's tag.

"Here, you know what," she said, "you boys do it. Something basic."

"Don't we need a VCR, too?" Nels said. "For your videos."

"I don't know," she said. "You know, you do it." She gave the money to Nels, who counted it almost solemnly. "I'll pull up with the van. Don't buy anything else. Hurry, *äkkiä*."

She turned, and she made her way back through the shelves, through the masses of music and movies, everything trying so hard to catch her eye, all that selling of sex, and she walked past the security guard without smiling, relieved for the door to slide open and for the music to cease as suddenly as it had begun. She hurried to the van, but when she climbed into the driver's seat the little kids were laughing, pretending each woman coming out the door was Simon's girlfriend, each man Paula's boyfriend.

"Don't do that," Pirjo said.

Impatient, she looped around the parking lot, past the office supply store, the pet store, the movie theater—poor Leena had once said that she wanted to work there, thinking United Artists was actually somewhere artists made art—and finally Nels emerged, the TV low in his arms, Simon skulking behind him, tossing his bangs to the side, and the little kids clapped and chanted, TV-TV-TV, and Pirjo said if they didn't quit she would bring it right back inside. On the ride home she turned up NPR so she couldn't hear them argue among themselves, watching them in the rearview mirror, Nels reaching out a wiry arm to stop the little girls from pinching. Simon just stared steadily out the window, ignoring everything; she wondered if he looked, like she did, at the lakes that were always visible through the windows of the wealthiest houses.

At home it was Nels who set up the TV, moving the old Finnish Bibles to a higher shelf, and they all stood and watched the one channel that came in, some local school channel, which was showing a middle school musical, girls in top hats, brandishing canes and short skirts.

Simon left the family room, came back with a video. "It's from the breadmaker," he said, and he put it in, and they sat and watched it, learned which equipment to use for which kind of bread, which flour.

"Do we even know where the breadmaker is?" Pirjo asked. "Has anyone seen it?"

"It still smells like peanut butter," Leena said. "I saw it in the garage."

The saleswoman talked, holding each part of the breadmaker up for the camera, with hands meant for rings, hands never meant to scrub half a tub of peanut butter from an expensive Christmas gift your kids had ruined.

"Why is everyone in here?" Pirjo asked. "Go, go, shoo. Go read some Dickens." By now Uppu had settled in on the floor, her neck bent up to the screen, her thumb hanging idly from her mouth. "Why does no one listen to me when your father isn't home? I said go. *Nyt, nyt.*"

She leaned over and searched for the eject button, finally succeeding in pressing it, and at that they all stood and wandered away, except for Uppu, who kept staring, waiting for the image to reappear.

When Warren came home from his speaking trip out east it was like she had brought home a small tiger, or a bomb. He didn't yell—Warren never yelled anymore, not since he'd nearly hit Nels and they had gone to parenting classes and he had been inculcated into the doctrine that loving your child was not enough—and now expressed everything, even anger, in disappointment.

He paced about the family room, putting his hand on the shelves he had built, picking books up, putting them back in.

"Waaraniemis have one," Pirjo said. "Jankkilas, too."

"We're not Waaraniemis."

"We're not Siltalas either," Pirjo said, trying to sound conciliatory. She could see the kids listening from the kitchen. She knew they were listening because they were cleaning—Simon was even mopping, but quietly.

"I just—" Warren sighed. "I had dinner with Tiina out east, you know. You should see her dorm room—her roommate has all these posters of rappers."

"Well," she said, "it only has a VHS anyway."

"VCR," Simon said, from the kitchen.

"VCR," she said.

"See," Warren said. He raised an eyebrow.

"It's just a TV," Pirjo said. She wanted to laugh, but she didn't want to make him mad.

"Then why are we still talking about it?"

"Well," she said.

"I don't want this shit in the house," he said, and she could see he didn't really mean to say shit, that it had just spilled out, but still she could feel the heat on her face, like the time he'd found her dabbing foundation under her eyes. Do you need to wear that? he'd said, and she'd soaped and soaped the makeup off, feeling like Lady Macbeth, but somehow worse for the very smallness of her sin. And she'd hated throwing it out, the expensive foundation, which she only had because it was part of the package with the skin cream at the mall, and she'd wanted to tell him that, to exonerate herself, but she didn't want to make it seem important. He turned and went into the kitchen, the bone of his bad knee cracking faintly as he walked.

"Jeez, Dad," Simon said.

"What?"

"Just, calm down," he said, working at a bit of scum on the floor, picking at it with his nail.

"Yeah?" Warren said, his voice edged with warning.

"I'm just saying." Simon stood and tossed his bangs away from his eyes, back over his cheek.

"Simon," Pirjo said.

"No, I'm saying. I say." Warren opened the fridge and ate a grape. The door of the fridge stayed open as he ate each grape, one by one. Everyone was quiet now—everyone had stopped moving, like it was choreographed, the five or six bodies in the kitchen all still.

"Just get out of my house," Warren said then, calmly.

Simon shrugged, his eyes rolling slightly, and set the mop almost tenderly against the counter. He strolled out past Warren, through the kitchen and through the family room, fighting with the sticking back door, and went out into the backyard. He walked out to the playhouse Warren had built for the little girls and knelt and crawled inside.

"That kid," Warren said.

"He's sixteen," Pirjo said, "we have to"—she paused, she

didn't want to sound like she was lecturing him—"we have to show more love." She could see that Simon was smoking now, the smoke rising through the window of the playhouse, something Simon always did to anger him. But she understood the smoking—so many of the church kids smoked because it was finally something they were allowed to do. She had a sudden vision of Simon when he'd been little, his hair a thick shock of dirty blond, wandering about the house in his diaper, eyes always upward, always peaked. He'd had a doll then—she'd insisted that all the kids have dolls, and not just white girls in pink bonnets—and Simon was forever misplacing Sugar in the sandbox, and he would walk around, full of adult worry, "Where's my Sugar? Where's my Sugar?" She and Warren would just roar, and poor Simon was hurt more by the laughter, and he would collapse and wail until someone fetched Sugar, and even then he would still look sad, only less lonely, as if glad that he had Sugar to share his sadness with. "Maybe you should go and talk to him," she said.

Warren turned and walked upstairs to their bedroom, slowly, but his heavy feet fell hard on the soft middles of the stairs. She wondered if Simon was cold outside—the weather looked nicer than it felt, the air still residually winter—and she hoped he would give up soon and come back in. She wanted to bring him a jacket, but she knew he wouldn't wear it. She finished his mopping, hoping he would come inside and see that she had done his chore, but he was as good as his father at winning by waiting.

At night now she watched the math videos with the family room door closed, pen and pencil in hand. The videos, she was pretty sure, were almost useless, the teacher an obvious actor, someone who looked good turning his back to the camera. After she had taken notes, redoing his problems again and trying to forget how he had reached the answer, she hid the remote behind the Finnish Bibles, like Warren wanted her to. She didn't like hiding it but it was a small enough concession, and she had only caught Julia looking for it the one time, and Julia had done an okay job of pretending to be searching for a book for class. Pirjo almost believed her.

A week passed this way, a week of Warren coming in from time to time to watch over her shoulder. She would take notes furiously, and Warren wouldn't say anything, leaving after a minute. He stopped talking about the TV entirely, until late one night when he said he was sure she would be a good teacher, and she said she already had been a great teacher, and then they both waited each other out until someone fell asleep first, maybe her.

But at one or maybe two in the morning she thought she heard Uppu at the door—they had never been good at getting the kids to sleep alone—and she waited for the hurt of light from the hallway in her eyes, Uppu's sleepy story about Hevonen jumping off a cliff, but no further noise came and Pirjo rose, like she always did when she wasn't sure, because there was nothing worse than being a parent and not being sure.

The hallway was empty, and there were the right number of lumps in the right beds, but still she walked downstairs, careful to step on the edges so they made no sound, the foyer light still on, and the living room light, too. She turned the corner into the kitchen and she saw Simon rising from an armchair pushed unusually close to the TV. The TV was still on, there was a low voice, a low thread of violins, a mountain moving across the screen. He eyed her, still standing.

"Is that the Lewis and Clark?"

"Yeah." He looked nervous still, but he sat back down.

"Is it any good?"

"They just made it to Shoshone territory." He leaned back a little. "Now they can get horses," he said. She came and stood behind the armchair, and the screen walked slowly over a sudden hill, back around it, twice, three times. She was cold—she was in only a long pink T-shirt that fell to her knees. Still she stood and watched, Simon's hand over the remote, at the ready, and she knew he was listening for the sound of Warren's bad knee. She stood until she had to sit, and then she pulled the computer chair over and she found some socks in the sock basket in the kitchen and she sat, arms wrapped around herself, until Lewis and Clark reached Fort Clatsop and the snow fell.

She didn't know how long it had been—her limbs were cold to the touch—and she rose and they moved the chairs back. They turned off the TV, and Simon took the video and she hid the remote back behind the Bibles. On his way out, Simon stopped and stood in the doorway. "Good night, chunk," she said. She wanted to hug him, but whenever she tried he always stood stiffly and waited for it to be over.

"Can I get a new nickname at least," he said.

"Oh, I don't mean that—you aren't even chunky anymore," she said, but he turned and stalked away, too tall, the thin hunch of male adolescence, she supposed. She was used to Brita's vanity, Tiina's slyness, Paula always saying the right thing but making you worry anyway, Nels hiding his feelings behind his silence—but Simon, with his variations on sarcasm and silence, was new to her. And he was so tall, so uncomfortable with himself still, and it was as if in growing he had surpassed her ability to reach him in any way—what was she to do with this thin, weedy thing that had somehow come from her and grown into this bitterness? She turned off the lights in the family room, and she closed the peanut butter jar in the kitchen, and wrapped up the bread, and put the milk back in the fridge, and turned out every light until at last the house was dark, like the rest of the street, like other houses.

When she awoke Warren was in one of his moods, marching in a circle around the house, with a pot on his head, Leena and Uppu and Anni marching behind him. Puuroa, stump-ah, they were chanting. On the stove Warren was cooking actual puuroa, and bacon.

When Warren was cheerful everyone became cheerful. The kids woke earlier than usual, and they were all at the table, reading the comics, waiting for food, knowing Warren would come with a big ladle to scoop the puuroa into everyone's bowl, knowing he would pour the milk with his arm raised up high, the milk falling three feet into the bowls, splashing out onto the table, silent Warren at last unsilent: open, Saturday Warren.

Pirjo had a concrete happiness, seeing the kids all at the table for once, almost everyone in the house at the same time, and Warren with his old puuroa routine, Simon joining the march as if he were little again. She wished Brita and Tiina hadn't gone away for school, Brita to Minnesota, where—Pirjo feared—she was just going to marry that Jimmy boy too fast, and Tiina out east, where church kids never went, but Tiina had begged. You can lose your faith anywhere, Tiina had said, which was obviously true. Movies and music and alcohol were everywhere—you had to trust your kids. She trusted her kids. They were good kids. She always felt that when she talked with the next-door neighbors—they had just put in a whole new security system that told them if their son tried to pull out of the driveway—and even when she talked to other church moms, whose girls got pregnant and married after tearful confessions, whose boys rode about town knocking down mailboxes, robbing convenience stores, making meth. Pirjo's kids led the choirs and the music camps, they asked forgiveness from each other, late at night—she had heard them.

It was late afternoon by the time the house had calmed down, Warren napping on the living room rug with Uppu rolled at his side, Paula babysitting down the street, Julia babysitting for a church family, Simon and Nels away at haps at Keranens', and there was the sound of Leena and Anni talking upstairs, playing something, probably trying every body product in the bathroom at once. Pirjo went into the family room, to the math videos. She took out the next in the series—about the quadratic formula—and she was going to sit down to watch it, she had her coffee and notebook and everything, when she thought of the video, the Lewis and Clark, and how all she wanted was to sit and have a quiet afternoon watching them make their way back across the country. Fine, she thought, I will, and she fetched it from the boys' room—always cleaner than she expected it to be, but dank with basement dew—and she went upstairs and put it in, feeling defiant, or maybe even proud. She wasn't surprised when the kids slipped in around her, watching the reenactors shoot off rifles and the journal of Meriwether Lewis scroll down the screen. A half hour passed before she felt Warren in the kitchen. He came over and stood behind the group of them.

"Isn't it crazy," she said, "to think they made it all that way to the ocean but then they just had to head back again."

He made an ambiguous noise but stayed to watch. "I like the dog," he said at last, and he grabbed the chair in front of the computer. He sat by her, and settled into it with his arms folded, and in silence they watched Lewis and Clark pass again by Beaverhead Rock, across the Mississippi, an hour gone like a dream upon waking. No one said anything when the credits began to roll—they all stood and Warren went into the kitchen and began to lay out tortillas for fajitas. He even whistled as he tore the plastic from the meat.

"I didn't get to see the rest of it," Simon said later that week. They were folding laundry together at the Ping-Pong table, the clothes stacked as high as her chest, a marathon of a folding session.

"Well, give it a week," she said. She did not feel like pushing it.

"Why? If Dad thinks it's okay—"

"If it's not a big deal, just wait." She felt a little uneasy about using Warren's logic, but it rang true.

"Okay," Simon said, and rolled his eyes.

"What, chunk?" she said.

"Just—okay."

"Okay," she said.

The call came the following Saturday night, saying that Simon had not showed up to do coffee lunch after the Youth Discussion at church. In fact, he had not even gone to the Youth Discussion. Jess Kariniemi had called, overly nosy as she was, pretending that she needed Simon to bring more cookies or goodies from home "if he's coming late" but, Pirjo sensed, really trying to find out where Simon was. "Is Simon okay?" Jess asked.

"Is Nels there?" Pirjo asked. "Can you just put him on, please?" For a few minutes Pirjo listened to the sound of the discussion in the background, delayed and broken up as it was by being broadcast from the sanctuary into the basement, and from the basement's speakers into her phone. "Girls, help us boys get into heaven," someone said, and then Nels was on. "What," he said.

"Where's Simon?" she asked. There was a pause. She wondered if he was eyeing Jess Kariniemi and the other workers in the kitchen. "Well," she said, "didn't he go with you?"

"I dropped him off."

"Really," she said. "Are you going to tell me where?"

"Mom," he said.

"You said you wouldn't tell? What was so important? Nels, honey, lovey, you aren't in trouble, but I have to know. I have to know where my children are. I have to know that he's safe."

"He's safe," Nels said, a laugh in his voice. "Okay, he's fine."

"Nels," she said, "you tell me right this minute."

"Uh," he said.

"The movies?" She tried to say it quietly, so that any of the little kids at home would not hear.

"I owed him a favor, okay, I'm sorry," Nels said. "I won't do it again."

"We'll talk when you get home," she told him briskly, and she hung up before he could say anything else. Her face was flushed. She felt a real and actual anger. She checked the clock—it was seven-twenty—the Youth Discussion had started at seven. It wasn't late. She stepped into the garage, where Warren had on thick plastic eyeglasses to protect himself from the buzz saw. She realized she didn't know what he was even building. It was always something. He would come home late from work, always behind on some deadline, and then he would fall asleep with the Bible, and spend his weekends fixing the house, tightening the cupboard doors, tearing out the doorway between the living room and dining room to build in an arch. Just take a day off, she always said, but he didn't know how.

"I'm heading out," she said lightly. "The little girls are upstairs."

"Okay," he said, and she got into their van, threw it into reverse, trying not to pull too hard out of the driveway. Simon, she prayed as she drove, you have such a good heart. I know it, I know it, she prayed. I saw you cry at your confirmation, she thought, and she hung on to that, that youthful contrition, that want for freedom and forgiveness. She hurried the van, impatient behind the SUVs heading out for Saturday dinner at family restaurants. Go, go, she urged them. She wanted to see Simon's face, to see if he felt guilty or not, to show him that he could not hide things. When she got to the movies, she parked at the back, walked as calmly as she could into the theater, following a dad with his kid on his shoulders. I'm just like him, she thought, just like anyone else going in to the movies. She entered and saw two booths behind glass, two young men sitting with microphones. There was a list of movies, too many, maybe ten—how was she to know which one Simon was in? Was Nels supposed to be picking him up afterward? She should have asked, she realized. She wondered if the theater was like an amusement park, if she could report that her kid was missing. She decided to see if they would stop her from going in, and she pulled at the second glass door, stepping into a giant catacomb of glass, the scent of popcorn sweet like rotting meat, the concession stand flanked by teenagers carrying unwieldy large drinks, rubbing up on each other, hands on shoulders, on hips.

She sat on a bench. No one else sat on benches—the benches seemed more gestural than functional—and some people looked at her funny, but she didn't care; she was good at not caring what other people thought. From watching the crowds she could see that Simon would have to come by her to leave the theater, and she felt like she was at the airport, waiting impatiently for him to cross past security and into her arms.

Twenty minutes passed, thirty. Her butt hurt from the bench. She was hungry, and she bought some popcorn, even though the price was some form of usury. She threw the receipt carefully away. Back at the bench, she went through her purse and cleaned it out, threw away all the old receipts and gum wrappers and Uppu's drawings from church, the drawing of every kid in their family, all labeled, in order of age, Brita with her boyfriend clinging to her stick-figure arm.

After a half dozen dirty-blond boys passed by, she saw Simon, turning a corner. He was walking beside a guy she didn't recognize, with short gelled hair—he was tan, or Hispanic maybe, she couldn't tell. She stood up, and she saw the other boy reach out and touch Simon, on the arm, the way boys never did, and then Simon looked up and when he saw her he became immediately red. She could see but not hear the guy ask if she was his mother, and she could see Simon say yes, and his friend began walking the other way, quickly, as if to avoid her, but she figured that was fine, she didn't have anything to say to him, and she waited for Simon to walk toward her, her heart sickly, nervous.

"Mom," he said, and he looked down at the star-spangled carpet.

"Simon," she said. "What are you doing here?" It was a stupid question, but it was all she knew how to say. He still hadn't looked up. It was really very loud, and she could hardly hear him over the music, over the streams of crowds. A girl ran screeching out of a hallway. A boy picked her up and began carrying her while she screamed in fake protest. Pirjo looked at Simon very carefully. She could see that he had done his hair.

"Mom," he said, "I didn't even want to see the movie." He

picked at a nail with his thumb. "Mom—" he said, "it was just that he—" and she saw what he was going to say, she knew with total and absolute finality what Jess Kariniemi had meant when she had asked, is Simon okay.

"We had to go somewhere," he said.

"Are you—" Her hands were literally shaking. "Don't say it," she said, "I need a minute."

Then his eyes began to tear at their edges and she pushed him by his elbow out the front doors and then they were outside, and there was the rush of the still-chilly spring. They stood on the grass at the side of the building, looking out at the dumpsters at the back, lit up by the parking lot lights.

"What am I going to do," he said, his voice cracking. "I don't know how to live," he said.

"Are you sure?"

"Mom," he said.

She wanted one of his cigarettes but couldn't bring herself to ask.

"What if I don't want to go, what if I want to stay?"

"What will you do?"

"I mean, I can just—" He shrugged. "It's a temptation like any other, right, I can still come to church."

"It's a very hard life," she said, not sternly enough. She wanted to say, It's an impossible life. She wanted to say, They will never like it and they will always look at you funny. Do you have to be this way? she wanted to say, but she made herself not say it.

"What am I supposed to do?"

She didn't know this answer. "I don't know," she said at last.

He kept touching his face, touching his hair, almost spastically. "I'm so scared," he said. "Dad will hate it. Dad will hate me."

"He's just your dad," she said. "Of course he still loves you," she said, but really she couldn't guess what Warren would say, if he would be quiet and calm and disappointed or if he would say something that would stick in Simon's mind forever. "Just remember—all sins, all sins can be forgiven," she said. "Even this one." She saw that his mouth had tightened into a firm frown, like it always did when he couldn't keep from crying, and she half wanted to hug him, to carry him as if he were not sixteen but two or three and had fallen asleep after a hard cry, and she would lay him down so gently he wouldn't wake, but only realize when he woke in his pajamas that he had been tucked in—and at the same time she wanted to shake him, to slap him. She felt slapped, she felt rejected, she felt like he had looked at the life she had made for him and he had spit on it.

She squeezed his arms and he collapsed into her, and she let him hug her, but she couldn't quite hug him back. She said his name, Simon, Simon, and she pitied him.


On the drive home it was as if there were no streets, no stop-lights, only Simon, his life playing back in her mind as she searched for the signs she hadn't seen, the signs in his life, in his face, in how he sat now in the passenger seat, his body turned away from her, his knee shaking like Warren's. Your child being gay was one of those things that happened to other peo-ple, like fires, car accidents where they needed the Jaws of Life. What had they done wrong? Science said there was nothing you could do—genetics—but that seemed like the worst answer of all. At church they said that gayness was a trial, like any other trial, any other temptation, and anyway all sin was the same in the eyes of God. But not in the eyes of man—that, that Pirjo had always known.

She was angry that now she had to be the mother with the gay son, the minister's wife with the gay son—always she would carry the burden of Simon with her, the shame of having birthed something that could not be happy in this world, like the shame of mothers with retarded children, the burden of having to love something society feared, something repulsive to the world. From now on people would always ask was he married, or was he dating, and each time she would have to keep her face still, she would have to be in control. She would never be able to admit her shame, and that was the greatest burden of all.

She pulled the van into their neighborhood, relieved to be home, scared to be home. On the street the same trees hung over the same telephone wires. Beyond the houses the lake laid staid and still. She parked the van near the garage and for a minute she and Simon sat, neither moving. At last she took her purse and made her way to the door but the house was dark, except for a blue twitch of light. "I'm home," she called out, but there was no answer. She turned the corner to see the girls in the family room. They did not even look up to see her enter, so steadfastly, so earnestly were they watching.

# PARTY BOY

NELS WENT TO a party.

He tried not to ask himself why.

Sure he was tired of his apartment. His apartment was a hole. His apartment was such a wasteland that new furniture changed exactly nothing. It had become a game, seeing how long he and Clayton could go without buying anything or cleaning anything. So far it had been three and a half months, and when he showered, the tiles were so filmed with dirt he felt only marginally cleaner.

His apartment was the reason Tricia didn't visit very much. When they saw each other now it was mostly on Saturdays. He would walk into Herralas' or Simonsons' or Muhonens', she would clear a spot for him on the floor, and she'd act like there weren't enough songbooks, so they could share. He hadn't even meant to date her, but now everyone said they were, so he supposed he was. It was fine, she was cute enough, but when he looked at her sometimes he felt like he could already see the mother in her, when her face would tire from the pregnancies. She wouldn't be fat, but her chin would be less defined and all of her motions would be too defined, from always grabbing at an escaping kid.

Maybe it was because of Tricia he went to the party. He'd been invited by a girl in orchestra, who played cello the way she talked, idly. "I never see you around," Bernie had said. The complaint was familiar—he never saw anyone who wasn't a believer—but the flirtation behind the accusation was pleasing.

"Maybe," he said.

But he surprised himself and went. Like on all Saturdays, he was supposed to go to haps, but he told Clayton he had studying to do, and when he heard Clayton's truck pull out of the driveway he took a shower. He found some clothes that looked careless. He brushed his teeth, just in case. He focused on walking hurriedly so he couldn't think about it, and even when he heard the music outside the door he didn't let himself falter, he just went in. It was a basement apartment, and the lights were garishly on, and there was a series of couches that people sat on, watching sports. Except for the music, it was awkwardly quiet. He guessed from the stink of things that everyone must have been high. This is what pot smells like, he told himself. He felt a strange stickiness beneath his feet and realized the entire carpet was pre-emptively covered in plastic, an odd maturity that anticipated immaturity.

Bernie pulled herself up from the couch when she recognized him. She brought him a beer. It amazed him how average everyone looked. Didn't they know they were at a party? He realized he also looked average. He tried the beer, and at first the stale smell revolted him, but he was good at mind over matter, good at plunging his hand into the garbage disposal when the sink was full of softened chunks of oatmeal and the pulps of peppers.

"So," Bernie said, "you're from . . ." She had a habit of waiting for people to finish her sentences.

He answered all of her questions without seeming too interesting. He'd gotten very good, over the years, at avoiding conversational paths that pointed toward the church. When she asked him, for instance, if he was going to the game on Friday, he said he already had plans and, anticipating a follow-up, asked about her. People liked themselves more than they liked to uncover his evasions. She was from St. Paul and her father worked at the library at the university and she had been trying to escape Minnesota her whole life but she never had. She said she hated the Midwest because it lacked radicalism. He asked if the insistence on moderation and middle age was its own radicalism. She took this to be clever, which he found a little overeager. When she talked he found himself staring at her breasts. She had the body of someone who didn't care what her body looked like—not heavy—but it was almost attractive, how she flung herself about. She couldn't, he thought, be less like Tricia, whose body was too polite to occupy space.

"God," Bernie said, "I feel like a sweaty mess. Do I look like a sweaty mess?" It occurred to him that she was nervous, too.

"You look great," he said awkwardly. He wasn't sure what he was supposed to say. His heart was drumming. But no one, ever, by looking at him, would guess that he was nineteen and the third oldest of nine kids and not supposed to listen to music with a beat. He went into the living room and leaned against the doorjamb and tried to look as if hell itself did not rest on what he did or didn't do that night.

\* \* \*

Someone dropped a stack of plates in the kitchen, and they broke. At this point in the evening it was hilarious, even to Nels. The heat on his face stretched back to his ears. Bernie poured more shots. "Shot number who knows," she said.

They played Never Have I Ever. The rules were not immediately clear to Nels, and he drank when other people drank, shaking his head when they shook their heads, laughing when they laughed. He spent everyone else's turn trying to think of what he would say, something that seemed, in its admission of having not done something, to admit to having done other, wilder things. When it was his turn he said, "Never have I ever"—inwardly unsettled at how long this list actually was—"made out in a movie theater." He did not mention that he had never really made out with his girlfriend, that even kissing her those few times had been risqué. He did not mention that he had never been to a movie theater, though he knew his other siblings had—Simon had invited him once, and Tiina, and once Tiina had told him that Brita used to go to the movies, but he didn't know if that was actually true. It was always him and Paula, at home, knowing where the others were but refusing to even ask.

By the time it came around to him again he was fully loosed from reality. He was undeniably drunk. I'm drunk, he wanted to say, gleefully, but he knew better. "Never have I ever—gone trick-or-treating," he said. It fell out of him. Whatever, he thought, they wouldn't get what it meant.

"Really?" someone crowed.

"We all have to drink," someone whined happily. Drinks were taken dutifully. Bernie looked at him funny.

He rose to go to the bathroom and felt a wave roll through him. Someone steadied him. He walked disjointedly to where the bathroom might be. He was interested in this feeling of drunkenness. He thought of the tests police gave people on the crime shows he used to watch at the neighbor's, like touching your finger to your nose or counting backward from ten. He was too drunk to assess his ability to perform these tests. He had to put his hand against the wall just to piss.

"So, no Halloween," Bernie said when he emerged from the bathroom.

"Nope," he said.

"Religion, I presume?"

"You could call it that." He shrugged and went to the back door and out onto the patio, where the beer was cooling. He struggled to pull a beer from the snowbank.

"No, really," she said when he came back in.

"Just a sticking point for my parents," he said, but he felt more nervous than he had all night. He didn't want to think about the church. He especially did not want to think abstractly about what sin he was doing while he was doing it—he wanted to reserve that for another time, for remorse. Of course that was exactly what you weren't supposed to do—sin with the expectation of forgiveness—but even as he drank his beer he landed upon a rationalization that satisfied him: he was only human. To err was human, to forgive was divine. Or something—he was drunk; he couldn't think. Yes, he thought, there it was. He was drunk; he couldn't be expected to think.


He awoke in his bed with a sour pit in his stomach. He made his way safely to the kitchen.

"So," Clayton said. Clayton himself broke rules—like listening to country—but he was the kind of church kid who was careful not to go too far. He was the kind of guy who would stop taking out movies from the library and throw out his CDs when he got married.

"Yeah," Nels said.

Clayton ate his cereal. He was big—he gave off an air of being immovable—but the weight was deceptive. Nels had seen Clayton on the farm, throwing ninety-pound hay bales without tiring, his cheeks pink with the effort but not a sound or heavy breath. The two cousins were nothing alike—the farm boy and the suburbs boy, Clayton always in some T-shirt espousing that a man never be separated from his truck, Clayton's jeans wide in the legs, baggy, belted. When he drove—beating two fingers against the steering wheel in time to country songs, raising a finger to say hi to passing drivers—he assigned one point for hitting roadkill and two points for hitting animals that were alive, but this might or might not have been a joke.

"You gotta shower now or we'll be late," Clayton said.

They drove out to the suburbs for church. Nels made Clayton stop once so he could vomit on the side of the road, but Clayton didn't say anything. During the sermon he sat next to Tricia and she offered him gum. He talked with her as briefly as was humanly possible. She was still in high school and was planning to apply to a nursing program, at St. Cloud State or maybe in Fargo, and he was pretending to be interested in premed when he just wanted to take cello lessons, and they talked about the premed stuff, the biology labs, which were endless. The chemistry courses, which had no foreseeable application. After the sermon, when they went out to lunch at a family diner, he sat with her and paid for her chicken strips. He could tell her friends were jealous.

On Thursday, Bernie called again.

"It's a stoplight party," she said. He looked that up online.

"Do you have a yellow shirt?" he asked Clayton. "Just to borrow for the night."

Clayton dug through a pile of clothes on his bed. He threw Nels a T-shirt advertising sunflower seeds. It was too big, but Nels tucked it in partway.

"Slowing down or speeding up," Bernie said, but she didn't seem dissuaded. Her shirt was green mesh. They bobbed next to each other in a room with all the furniture pushed to the sides. She pressed her back up against him and he took a step back. He nodded his head harder, as if the music meant something. People kept getting excited about each song that came on, and he put his hand in the air and tried to look excited, too. Everyone mouthed words, and he kept his head turned toward the floor. It must have been an hour later, maybe more—he was doing some kind of dance, some kind of head bobbing with some girl or, at least, near some girl—when Clayton appeared in the doorway of the room. He was wearing a Twins cap. He had a red cup in his hand.

The room was dark, but Nels worried that shame was visible in the dark.

"You left your phone," Clayton said. He dug in his pocket for it. "That girl called again. Bernie. She wanted you to bring a mixer, so I brought Coke."

"Oh," Nels said. He felt relieved, then excited. "Nice, man, nice. What's that," he said, pointing to the cup.

"Coke."

"Oh," he said.

Bernie appeared. "Your friend," she said to Nels. "Did you know"—she was bemused—"he's an actual, like, real, live Republican?" She pushed at Clayton, but he didn't even rock back. "You're kinda cute," she said to Clayton, "for a Republican who solves centuries of ingrained ideologies with guns. Come on," she said, and she took his hand. She pulled at him, and, genial Clayton, he followed. Nels sat on a couch. "I'm so drunk," a girl said next to him. "I can't drink this," she said, so he downed it, and it burned brightly, he felt the booze churn in his stomach.

When Nels finally rose to get another drink, Clayton was sitting in the living room. Bernie was on his lap. Clayton looked uninterested in the fact that Bernie was sitting on his lap. "Please," she was saying to Clayton. She made a moue. "Just one little sip," she said, and she pressed the lip of her cup to his mouth. Clayton pushed the cup away.

"Yo," Nels said.

"What's up," Clayton said. He lifted his cap in a kind of salute. Then he managed to stand with her in his lap. He set her on the floor. He didn't seem angry, just bored. Nels admired him, for being bored with the scenario. It reminded him of his father, how his dad bolstered his intelligence with silence.

"What's up with him," Bernie said as he left.

"He's from a farm," Nels said, as if this explained anything. "Cows. Not very lively," he said. He drank with a fervor.

That weekend at haps Tricia caught him by the cheese and crackers. Everyone else was singing in the living room—here as a flickering candle, has been my life of faith—and Nels was ladling himself more punch. It was sickly sweet and tasted of childhood.

"Are you going to Pelkie Ski Days?" she said. "I was thinking . . . we could borrow Clayton's truck and go out together."

"Finals, you know," he said.

"Well, anyway," she said. "Come over for Tyler's birthday. He's one—big day," she added. She was the oldest of ten.

"Going to let him just dig into the cake?" he joked. It felt strange, that domesticity was what they had to talk about. He had a brief vision of Uppu when she was small, clawing happily at the whipped cream. He said he would go.

When he got home from haps it was early still, barely midnight. He and Clayton had ditched early, hadn't stuck around for the board games. Nels was falling asleep on the couch when Tiina called to say that Brita was pregnant.

"Crazy, isn't it?" Tiina said. "Crazy, crazy, crazy."

"Congrats, man," Clayton said. "Gonna be an uncle." Clayton had fourteen nieces and nephews and only four of his siblings were married.

"Yeah," Nels said. The news made him edgy. Brita had just been married four months ago, and he felt like he was still adjusting to that, the idea of her being married, a wife—those adult words still felt odd in his mouth. It seemed to presage his own life, when he would be calling Brita to say Tricia was pregnant. The thought made him ill. Who contemplated these things at nineteen? "Wanna go out?" he asked Clayton, but Clayton was nearly asleep on the couch, his chin flush with his chest. Nels walked the streets, pushing his pace, trying to wear something off, or something out. He realized he wanted Bernie to call him, or maybe he just wanted to be somewhere loud, someplace where he couldn't hear himself think.

He called Bernie and in twenty minutes he was downtown, and she got him into a bar through the back door. The place was jammed and the speakers popped things inside him, in his ears, in his blood. He shouted things at Bernie and she shouted things back at him and they had something to drink. He had a shot, two shots. He jumped up and down. He felt not deadened by the noise, not annoyed, not smothered, but alive—there was a strange synchronicity to the dancing, like everyone raising their hands to give forgiveness in church. There was a contagion to the movement. He recognized people from the stoplight party, and he felt very close to them, they seemed like great people. Why hadn't he been friends with them before? What were their names? John, Jenny? He didn't know. He didn't care. He felt a hundred old happinesses rise in him as one. How had this desire—to move like an animal, with crude and sudden movements—waited in him so long? He didn't even mind when Bernie pressed against him, he let it be part of the night. He had another shot and it boiled less urgently in him, mixing more smoothly with what he was feeling, pushing him further and further into the surrounding sound.

Outside the feelings dampened sharply with the shutting of the door behind them. Bernie stood and looked at him expectantly and he felt it would be rude not to kiss her, so he did. In the brief seconds they had been out of the bar her mouth had managed to become cold, and he was reminded of putting his pillowcase in the freezer in the summer. He pulled away. "I gotta go," he said. She didn't disagree.

On the walk home he had to stop to throw up, vomiting into a window well because it had the aspect of depth, even though as he did it he could see, through the basement window, people playing video games. They saw him vomiting. A guy yelled, "Sick, man, do that somewhere else," and gave him the finger. He wiped snow around his mouth and tried to make his way home. He'd left his jacket in the bar but he didn't want to go back in to get it, and instead he walked home in his T-shirt, and when he stepped through the door to his apartment Clayton was reading a book, some western.

"Dude," he said, "you were out there with no coat on?"

"Just a short walk," Nels said, focusing hard on sounding not drunk.

"There's something on your shirt."

"Oh," he said. He wiped at frozen puke.

In his bed he couldn't fall asleep. What he had done did not feel real. He tried to recount the night deliberately—I snuck into a bar after haps, and at the bar I had shots and danced. He remembered suddenly that he had kissed Bernie.

No more, he thought, and he shook his head. Now you've done that. Now no more. Still he couldn't fall asleep, until he remembered he hadn't gone through the Benediction, and he thought through each phrase with his hands folded. But the memory kept waking him, and he stood and shook his hands violently. He did ten push-ups. He opened the window and let the cold air in, and laid down on the floor, remembering to turn onto his side, in case he vomited in his sleep.

He told Clayton.

"Can I—" he said. They were in the kitchen and Clayton was rinsing a staled cup of coffee. "Can I have it taken care of?" he asked. He kept his voice light.

"All sins forgiven in Jesus's name and precious blood," Clayton said. They didn't look at each other. Clayton poured coffee into his hardly rinsed cup.

Nels left for class. When he walked he felt so full of something—hope, maybe—he wanted to run. The sky was the same stubborn white, but he felt cheerful about the snowbanks and about the sidewalks packed down but not cleared. The iced air woke him up, made him feel clean and alert. He sat in the back of the lecture hall and wondered about all the people sitting there, bored, trying to figure out who they had a chance with. He felt bad for them, for the limits of their experiences, for the fragility and infrequency of their happiness. They did not even know, he thought, the kind of happiness they wanted.

He remembered the bar, the surge of sound. It had come and gone. He thought maybe he would invite Bernie to church. No, he decided, that was weird. He wondered if he should call her at all, clarify what had happened the night before.

But wasn't this the whole college gambit? You had absurdist experiences. You were allowed to and even supposed to, was how Bernie would see it—that was how the world saw it. That was how the world did college. Bernie would move on.

Up in front the professor wandered on about buffers, equal amounts of acids and bases. Like blood, she said. Blood is a buffer, so that if you are exposed to acid, you have bases in your blood to neutralize the acid. Okay, Nels thought. He tried to fix the thing in his brain but he already felt it slipping.

He went with Tricia to the Mall of America. She wanted to do things—the roller coasters, as if the tickle-belly of the ride was exciting, when it was only the context, only the sight of shoppers on the third floor that made the spin and drop of interest. Then it was the photo booth, where she let him fight to give her bunny fingers, so all their pictures were blurred, her face showing her pleasure at being teased.

Then she wanted him to try on new jeans, so they went to the same store everyone went to and Tricia mocked all of the innuendo on T-shirts—"Tacky," she said—and she began browsing the racks. He was waiting for her to find the right blue of jeans when Bernie appeared from the dressing room in a too-short dress.

"Nels!" she said, clearly pleased, and she came and gave him a hug and he could feel her body. She draped her hand on his arm, chattering, saying did he hear about Jenny sleeping with John again.

He felt Tricia eyeing him.

"Oh," Nels said, "this is Tricia."

"Oh!" Bernie said. Her face became red but she stayed resiliently cheerful.

Tricia smiled without showing her teeth. Nels saw how Bernie saw her, slightly infantile—her T-shirt was plain and white—and average in every way, in what she wore, in how she did her hair. It occurred to him that almost everyone in the church dressed this way, as if dressing like a more modest version of everyone else would keep them both the same and apart.

"Listen," Bernie said, "you should both come tomorrow night."

"I don't know," Nels said. "We're going to be at Tricia's place, I think. Tyler's birthday?"

"That's Sunday," Tricia said. "After church."

"You don't want to miss it, though. It's going to be at John's again, but rumor says it's going to be a kegger."

"A what?" Tricia asked. The way she said this, as if it weren't an embarrassing question, made him wonder if she already knew what it was.

"You know," Bernie said awkwardly, "a keg." She clearly lacked the ability to be cruel, wide open as the opportunity was. "You should come," she said to Tricia.

"Yeah," Tricia said.

He walked with Tricia slowly around the racks. She held up pants that clearly would never fit him. "I had it taken care of," he said. "Clayton," he added.

"Okay," she said, "I get it," but she wanted to leave. She didn't want a pretzel from the pretzel stand, like she always did. He dropped her off at home and he didn't go inside to say hi to her parents. Two of her little brothers waved from behind the glass door.

\* \* \*

Tricia told him she didn't want to be with him anymore. "You make me a worse believer," she explained over the phone. "It makes me doubt." She didn't like to doubt things. He didn't go to Tyler's party.

"All the Marjanens are super straight like that," Clayton said.

The semester passed without him seeing Tricia outside of church, and without him seeing Bernie outside of class. At haps he had the feeling that all of the girls were staring at him; in orchestra Bernie had stopped poking him in the back with her bow, and they said hello and good-bye the way people who are trying to avoid each other do, with exaggerated enthusiasm. He got his usual top-of-the-middle grades—he had long since dealt with his sisters' overachieving by not really trying, though he was aware of this defense mechanism—and he spent his free time with Clayton, playing the video games his mom wouldn't have let him play at home. He ate grilled cheese sandwiches; he got skinnier still.

By the time he went home for Christmas break, he felt only embarrassment when he thought about the semester, how typically he'd behaved, going away to college and sneaking off to parties. But almost as proof of their faith in him no one asked and he didn't offer, and this made it still more difficult to offer.

He came back after break to find Bernie waiting where his stand partner usually sat. She looked better—her outfit called less attention to itself.

"I just wanted to say sorry," she said.

"What for?" He took his cello out of its bag, to keep things casual. He felt nervous.

"I made things all weird."

"No," he said, "not at all, I'm not even with Tricia anymore—it's not a big deal."

"Yeah," she said. "I mean, I'm dating someone now."

They went out for coffee, to a family diner where the waitress called them sweetheart and asked too frequently if they needed warm-ups. They ordered pecan pie, and Bernie told him about the guy she was dating, and asked what had happened with Tricia, and for a long swig of coffee he considered an easy lie but then he figured it didn't matter, and he told her everything, he told her about the church, about growing up. He listed all the things he couldn't do. He told her about modesty and restraint and not tempting yourself.

"It's just always easier not to do stuff," he said, "than to think you can handle something, and then before you know it you're doing the next thing you weren't supposed to be doing."

"Yeah," she said. He couldn't tell if she thought he was crazy or not. He showed her pictures on his phone from Brita's wedding, and she learned all their names in order, reciting them almost as fast as he could—Brita-Tiina-Nels, Paula-Simon-Julia, Leena-Anni-Uppu—and he told her which instrument each of them played.

"You all look alike," she gushed. "The same eyes."

"No," he said, "not once you know us."

He kept hanging out with Bernie. He felt comfortable around her now. She knew his secret, and he could tell she kept it. She didn't invite him to things, but he would go over to her apartment—so large and spacious she didn't even use one of her rooms, the fortunes of an only child visible everywhere—and they went through her cello CDs and she never made him look at her other music, even though he kind of wanted to.

"Listen," she said one night, "my birthday's next Thursday and I want you to come. Other people are coming, there's going to be stuff there and everything, but you don't have to do any of it, obviously."

"It's fine," he said, and he went. When he got there he realized how many friends she had—she went to everyone else's parties, and so they were all obliged to come to hers. She served drinks from a cooler, a mix of whiskey and beer and pink lemonade, and Nels could smell it on everyone's breath, sweet and heavy at the same time. Bernie gave him a cup that was pure lemonade, and it was so sharply sweet he coughed, and he wished he were just drinking water in a clear cup, without pretense. Someone appeared with a cake, and the group sang, remarkably out of tune, no one able to agree on a starting pitch. Everyone seemed to be having more fun than he was—nothing was funny to him. He didn't feel like watching people dance. He wished Bernie hadn't given him the lemonade; he wished she didn't know he wasn't supposed to dance. He felt like leaving, but he had to look like he was having fun so that she'd think it was possible to have fun without drinking and dancing.

Now he was sulking. He made small talk with people he knew vaguely, but they were talking about a TV show he'd never seen. This made him feel still worse—he never knew if he should pretend or not, or try to change the conversation. He kept his eye on Bernie, and when he was sure she was out of the room, he put on his jacket. He went into the kitchen, and from a number of bottles on the counter, he took a bottle of amber-colored liquor. Rum. He held the bottle like it had been his all along and strolled calmly out the door. No one waved goodbye or asked why he was going, and by the time he was out in the street he felt stupid and angry. As he walked he could hear sounds emanate out of other people's houses—the spurts of televised gunfire, a louder party, complete with stragglers smoking on the porch. A loner played the harmonica on his back porch, badly.

In his apartment he took out a mug with a drawing of deer. He poured an inch of rum. He sniffed it; it stank. Clayton came out of his room.

"How was the birthday?"

Nels took a swig. His eyes teared sharply and he coughed. "Try it," he said.

Clayton lumbered over. He picked up the bottle and studied it.

"Don't you ever wonder?" Nels said.

Clayton sniffed the top of the bottle. "What makes you think I haven't?"

Nels took another swig from his mug, larger this time. "A toast," he said, "to—" He wanted to think of something inappropriate, funny, make Clayton loosen up a little. "To my dad, good old Warren Rovaniemi, who talks about his kids' sins in his sermons. Bring this one up, Dad, see what they think."

Clayton tipped his head from one heavy shoulder to the other.

"This one's to—Howard Pelto," Nels said. He poured another. "Neil Ojala."

"Buddy Laho," Clayton suggested. His tone was flat.

"Good one," Nels said. "Here," he said. He poured some into another mug.

Clayton picked up the mug and sniffed the rum. He tasted it, and his eyes, squinting, teared a little. "Well," he said. "Tastes like booze, I guess."

"Why," Nels said, "when did you have it?"

Clayton shrugged.

"Farm boy," he said. And he downed it, coughing. It wasn't until his second mug that he began to laugh—they both began to laugh. Nels felt light and easy. His yoke was easy and his burden was light.

When they woke the next day they didn't speak of it. Nels was the one to clean the bathroom and the shower, which, after some heavy vomiting, badly needed it. They went to a Youth Discussion out in Menahga, and to church, and even to Communion, the taste of wine at Communion bizarrely familiar and now not unpleasant. When they drove to and from church events they still listened to Clayton's country music, and they still turned the radio to a news station before they turned into the church's parking lot.

"So I guess it doesn't matter?" Nels said.

"What doesn't matter?" Clayton said, and they left it at that.

Fine, Nels decided, he would put it from his mind—it was just one night, one thing, he thought. At some point he would bring it up to someone, have it forgiven—not Clayton; a believer could not forgive sins committed with another believer—but he put it off in his mind, an unpleasant duty, a task for another time. For a few weeks he did his life, and he went to his classes, and he passed exams, and from time to time he would almost forget, but he would be falling asleep at night, turning, and he would think, What is it, what am I forgetting? And he would remember about the drinking. During the sermons he almost wished the ministers would talk about drinking, mention it as a direct sin, so he could feel that specific remorse, but when they talked about sin he had the feeling they were referencing sins much smaller than his own. He felt he was being allowed to get away with it.

"Each sin brings about a hardening of the heart," Buddy Laho said. "Each sin hardens your heart a little more, until one day it feels nothing at all, one day you sin and then—it doesn't even bother you." Nels felt this was probably true. It was probably why he could sit there and think about the drinking and still do nothing about it.

For weeks he felt slightly anxious. He skipped lectures. He and Bernie still went out for coffee sometimes but he felt embarrassed, and he stopped picking up her calls. He got moved down a chair in orchestra. When his mom made her occasional calls he didn't answer those, either. He thought of who he could call—he didn't want to call his parents, who would worry it would happen again and who would make him transfer to a Michigan school. He didn't want to call Brita, who only talked about being pregnant. He didn't want to call Tiina, who everyone knew was going off her own deep end, dating an unbeliever and acting like she wasn't. He didn't want to call Paula, who had probably never had a sinful thought in her life. He didn't want to call Simon, whom he had never had a serious conversation with in his life. The little kids were still little kids—he didn't want them to know that these sins even existed.

"What's the matter with you?" Clayton said. He was gone from the apartment more now. Nels heard him come in late at night, sometimes, but he didn't ask.

"I don't know," Nels said. He was moody.

He borrowed Clayton's truck and drove out to Tricia's. At the door her dad let him in, shook his hand. He had to say hello and God's Peace to each of their little kids. There was something protracted and painful about this farce. Tricia was in her bedroom, reading. He stood at the door to her room, aware that everyone was listening. He had never seen her bedroom; there were two sets of bunk beds. She sat on the bottom of one of the bunks. On the walls behind her bed she had taped up pictures of actors, neatly cut out from magazines. She saw where he was looking.

"I've never seen any of their movies," she said hastily. "They're just cute." Her face was red.

They walked around her neighborhood. The homes were all split-level ranches. It was chilly, but there was the smell of dirt again, and the snow had melted except in a few spots.

They walked to a nearby park, sat on the swings. Around them parents with only two children monitored their kids' every move, hanging behind them as they climbed rope ladders, reaching toward them as they slid down poles. One mom kept following her son with a tissue, wiping his nose.

"These poor kids," he said.

"Yeah," she said appreciatively. They agreed that there was something sad about families that small, where the parents foisted all their hopes onto one or two kids.

From the swings he told her things. When he talked he looked out at the houses and not at her. He told the very worst of it, the very worst of himself. He told her about lying to her before, he told her about kissing Bernie, dredging up feelings he was only newly remembering. He didn't even have to ask for the forgiveness; she put her hand out and from the swings they held hands. She gave him the forgiveness and he didn't cry. They walked more, around and around. They talked about houses, about whether they wanted to live in a brick house with the bricks painted white. They both wanted a garden. They both wanted a dog, and no cats. He wanted a big dog; she wanted a little dog. Two dogs.

He wanted to kiss her but it didn't seem appropriate.

It was months before he realized how hard Clayton was drinking. Nels might never have realized it, except he went in to borrow a T-shirt and he smelled it, that strange fermented stench. He picked up Clayton's laundry from the floor and began sniffing it, and it was only when he opened the window to let in air that he saw the bottles, a half-drained fifth of vodka, a six-pack, an unopened pint of whiskey.

For a few weeks he didn't mention it, just kept his eye on Clayton, paying attention to when Clayton disappeared into the bedroom and when he came home at night. When he finally brought it up, Clayton shrugged.

"I'll straighten out," he said. "I'm going into the army, anyway." But he didn't straighten out. He was drinking now just to fall asleep. He was keeping all the booze openly out on the counter, and in the fridge.

"I should leave," Nels told Tricia. It's not good for my faith, he wanted to say, but he didn't want to admit that.

"He's family," Tricia said, so he lived with Clayton for another year, but when he and Tricia decided to get married he did not ask Clayton to stand for him, and by the fall of the wedding, they were hardly speaking.

"I thought it wasn't a big deal," he said once to Clayton.

Clayton shifted his heavy shoulders and said nothing.

During the wedding ceremony, Nels could see Clayton sitting patiently. He'd put on a suit and though he'd gained weight, especially in his face, he looked decent. When Nels went to shake his hand in the receiving line he could not be sure, but he thought he picked up the faint smell of whiskey on Clayton's breath. At the very end of the receiving line was Bernie. Her curly hair was down and she wasn't wearing any makeup. She said nice things about the ceremony and his father's sermon. These were probably lies, he thought, but it was nice of her to say them.

At the reception Bernie and Clayton sat and ate together.

He pointed it out to Tricia as they ate their casserole. "While there's life, there's hope," she said. There was another sermon during the reception. His family sang. Her family sang. They ate their wedding cake, and again and again he told himself this was right, this was good.

# WE SINNERS

THE KARVONEN BOYS were in town and Tiina didn't mean to dress carefully, but she did. All of her sisters did, even Brita, who was pregnant again; that was the effect the Karvonens had. Tiina knew it was pathetic to care, but there was not a single church girl who had not imagined marrying a Karvonen boy.

After the service she stood with her sisters in the back, pretending not to look at them. The Karvonens had hair cropped close, and they all wore collared shirts in pale, prudent tones.

"So beautiful," Julia said.

"Whatever," Tiina said. "They're just people." She checked her phone for messages from Matthew.

"If they're just people, go talk to them."

"Fine," Tiina said. She resisted the impulse to fix her hair. As she walked she was aware that everyone knew she was approaching them, so she walked still more quickly.

"Hey," she said.

"God's Peace," they said, but she couldn't say it back. She

nodded at them. She felt unsure if she should actually shake their hands. She shook their hands and their hands were firm and broad.

"How's Detroit treating you?" she asked. She didn't really want to know. She assessed them—they really were grossly good-looking—and she tried to convince herself Matthew was just as good-looking, but this pretense failed.

"I always forget what a small congregation this is," the least handsome said dully. She adjusted her bag on her shoulder. She checked her phone again.

They discussed where haps was going for lunch.

"Isn't that where we went last time?" they said to one another. They didn't look at her. Was it the one near the freeway exit? Remember that waitress who wanted their picture? When they laughed they denied her the full strength of their teeth, their full powers.

She excused herself from the circle and nearly walked into Arnie Aho. "Trying to catch a Karvonen, eh?" Arnie said. The Karvonens could hear him, she knew. She could have strangled him with his own belt, with the brass buckle, but she smiled.

There's nothing to be embarrassed of, she thought as she walked out to the front lawn. What do I want with a Karvonen? She would not think of it. It was futile to give the Karvonens, or Arnie, or anyone at church, even an extra minute of thought. But all during the ride to the restaurant she kept thinking about Arnie, with his uncomfortably full mustache and his cowboy boots, talking about her to his wife. If he only knew, she thought—she'd told her family that next week she was going to a conference, when there was really no conference, when really she was flying out to Matthew. In only one week she would leave the church. She felt bad about the lying but lies had to be told, so that truths could be told. This was how Matthew put it. He was the great justifier of her greatest indiscretions.

She half wanted to tell Paula and Julia what she was doing and half never wanted them to know. I'm sorry, she wanted to say preemptively, but she wasn't sorry. She was glad. She was glad she was going to get out and be done with the Karvonens. Be done with the church, with its sad girls chasing sad boys, its sad fathers and mothers. Be done with Arnie, the carpenter that he was, trying to raise his kids in a trailer, his wife wide in the hips now, wide and weary, with the Farrah Fawcett hair she hadn't changed since her wedding. Tiina had a vision suddenly of his wife driving her home; Tiina had been babysitting. Beth and Arnie had come home early. The whole ride Beth had chattered—she was always nervous, laughing a little too easily, which made Tiina like her—and when they pulled into the driveway Beth had gone to reach into her purse to pay Tiina. Beth's hair had spilled into her purse, the Farrah Fawcett hair shaking, and then Tiina had realized Beth was not looking but crying, and Beth had told her she'd had a miscarriage at the restaurant. How did miscarriages happen, Tiina wondered now. Was Beth eating her chicken chimichanga and then she had felt a pain? Did she go to a bathroom and see the bleeding, like a period but heavier, milkier? Did it hurt? But Beth had only said, God giveth and God taketh away, and she'd gone back to searching her purse.

"Poor Beth," Tiina said aloud.

"What?" Julia said.

"Oh," Tiina said, "nothing, nothing," and she sighed as they pulled into the restaurant.

But when the week had passed, and the right lies had been told at the right time, and the conference clothing had been exchanged in the airport bathroom for a revealing top, she felt afraid. She felt no thrills of liberation. She'd painted her fingernails a bright green—tropical tango—and when she walked toward the baggage claim she knew the nails were a puerile rebellion against the church, and when she saw Matthew, his haircut too new so it rode up above his ears, she wanted to crawl back to the plane. When Matthew saw her he was suddenly eager and she was suddenly shy. She saw that they had each thought too hard about what they wore.

They made it back to the house he shared with two friends. His bedroom was too nice for an undergraduate, as if he were prematurely middle-aged, with actual bookshelves and a desk with a matching cherrywood chair. She felt tired and anxious but they had sex, as if sex were the only way to fix those things, even though it didn't. She tried not to think about the Karvonens, about their bodies. "Trillium," he said, and he kissed the inside of her palm. He was happy and he wanted her to be happy. In his very countenance was his confidence that her visit was a good idea, that she would not get caught, that she was going to leave the church.

His happiness was contagious; she became happy. They took a shower, and she used his sulfate-free shampoo, and she didn't let this annoy her, that he was someone who took a stand against shampoos that foamed—he was the one, after all, who had taught her how to open a wine bottle, who'd explained Yoko Ono to her, who knew that when she walked in a movie theater she looked behind her back. He was tall, taller than her dad and her brothers, and from certain angles—when his hair was longer and hid his ears—he had an old-fashioned handsomeness, an actual aquiline nose and widow's peak. She reached for a towel, but he made her switch. "This one is fluffier," he said. He wrapped her in it. Downstairs in the garage someone had begun to play a guitar, a slow, steady strum, the chords minor and crass.

And so they spent two days in bed, a bruise forming slowly at the top of the inside of her thighs, and she felt validated, like she had some concrete proof of what her transgressions had bought her. The plane ticket—paid for, when she allowed herself to recall it, by Matthew—faded from her mind. She lived as if she had come from a family that did not have to be explained, like a little kid playing dress-up, playing that she had no past, playing a future loosed from any past. In return, he spoiled her. He felt, she thought, that she had somehow lost out in the fight for attention among all her siblings, and he was almost maniacally trying to make up for her childhood of split candy bars and a teddy bear for a pillow, and he seemed intent, most of all, on proving how great it was to be only two, only the two of them, young, him with big loan money and the audacity to spend it. She couldn't help but love it; her vanity was finally being coddled, and after years of Finnish modesty and minimalism, his grandiosity was a relief.

By the third night at dinner she had given in entirely to the feeling that this was what life outside the church had to offer her, and it was good. Someone came to talk to them about the wine—the sommelier, as Matthew called him—and she felt very above her family, above believers who only ate out, if they ever did, at an Italian family restaurant where all the grainy photographs of kitchens were mass-produced in Milwaukee. She knew somewhere in her mind that they weren't so cultured themselves, that Matthew's pretense at money was just that. True, his parents had come from old money. His grandparents, or maybe great-grandparents, had invested in General Electric before it was General Electric, and had once built themselves houses with whatever useless accoutrements they desired—a greenhouse, a steam room, an elevator—but at some point in his childhood they had made some bad real estate decisions and lost it all. Now he tried to make up for the superiority of their past money with the superiority of his education—he believed in knowledge for knowledge's sake, he gave her Greek histories, and wrote her cards in epic verse.

Over dessert, for instance, he talked about the problem of translating Isaiah 7:14, how "virgin" had been translated incorrectly in the Septuagint—in the original Hebrew it was really "young woman," possibly meant euphemistically, but not necessarily so, and look at what had come from that, that one mistranslation. By the time of the Gospels, it was too late! She said she didn't know what the Septuagint was. He said she should really be studying these things. He said she would feel better about everything, once she saw how many holes there were.

In turn she told him about the theory of performative speech. "So in class," she said, "she's explaining what it is, like the idea that there are these kinds of language, pieces of our speech, that aren't really fact or truth, they're just statements we make that do a thing." As she talked about it she had the sensation of being not quite there, an awareness of talking about performative speech just to be the kind of person who talked about performative speech. But she liked when they talked like this, their big world, big theory ways.

"Austin calls it constantive speech," she went on, "you know, like saying 'I do' at a wedding or naming your baby. So of course," she said, "people are talking about examples of this, and of course, what do I think of—"

"The church," he said.

"Forgiving sins," she said, "yeah."

"Or leaving the church," he said pointedly.

She set her fork on her plate in the five o'clock position. She gave what she hoped was a wistful smile. "I have what, three, four more days here," she said. "Not yet."

"Tiina." He said her name like an American, like she was an ordinary Tina. She swirled her wine in the glass. She thought she detected, as the sommelier had told them, a buttery finish.

"You want to go downtown tomorrow?" she said at last. "I want to go downtown."

"Tiina," he said again.

"Let's go to the bookstore. Let's sit an entire day in the store and read a whole book, then we don't even have to pay for it. Man, we used to do that all the time. Go to the bookstore after church, just sit in the kids' section on the carpet and read."

"I'll buy you books," he said.

"You're not buying me books."

"Why not?" he said.

"I don't buy you things."

"Leave the church. You don't have to buy me anything."

"It doesn't work that way," she said. They were talking quietly, casually, but she felt nervous, like she always did when the church came up. She was suddenly cold.

"Everything works that way. Everyone's just in it for themselves. Everyone has totally selfish reasons for being in the church, when it comes down to it. Basic, primal reasons, like it means they have safety, or a husband, or whatever."

"Some people actually believe, you know," she said. She said this to test if, as she said it, she knew it was true. She knew it was true.

"Stop seeing it their way. Be selfish already."

"The way you're being selfish. The way you just want me to be free of it all," she said.

He finished off his drink. "Everybody wants something," he said, almost sadly.

They did all of their normal things. They went to movies and went to bars to talk about the movies. They slept in. The sex became less impassioned and more conscientious, where he was a careful lover and she was careful to be appreciative of his conscientiousness. Actually she was sometimes bored, knowing always what they were going to do next. His preferences were too clear and too well formed, and it worried her that she knew his wants so well already when, she felt, so much remained for him to realize about hers. She was of the school of mostly faking it. Her friends said not to do that, but she didn't believe them when they said they didn't—what else could you do, in that moment?

Once the fanatical need for sex had worn itself out some, the objective of leaving the church became paramount. The barrage began. Matthew had long taken it upon himself to initiate her into the art of atheism, but now he threw himself wholeheartedly into convincing her that Laestadianism was, as he put it one afternoon: one, like all religions, entirely manmade and fabricated; two, as religions went, a particularly painful form of emotional abuse; and three, practically speaking, an unlivable lifestyle in the modern-day world.

It was nothing she hadn't heard before, but there was an urgency to it. "Did you know," he said, "Laestadius had more kids than your family—he beat you guys." They were sitting in his living room, laptops searing their thighs. "Laestadius, twelve; Rovaniemis, nine."

"Yeah, well, the prize is poverty," she said. "I take that back," she said. "I don't really mean that."

"His poor wife," he said. He was reading something very carefully. "The poor woman. She had twelve children, but three of them died. I wonder if she knew what she was getting into, following this man as he started this religion."

"What if she was in love with him? Do you ever think about that," she asked, "people in the past marrying for love? What if when she met him she heard bells?" Her mother had said that, once, about her father. It was, in fact, the only thing she had ever said about meeting him. Tiina herself had never heard bells. She and Matthew had been friends, for a few years—she was a flirt, and it was in her nature to have friends who were boys—and it had been so clear he liked her, and it was so powerful, being liked like that, and really his occasional officiousness was justified. He was actually brilliant; his mom had told her his IQ score. And he was endlessly patient about the church, and he came to the Sunday school Christmas program, and Easter, and her sisters liked him, even if they guessed what was going on. Her parents had eyed him warily, and made sure she knew that men and women couldn't ever be just friends. I know, she'd said, managing not to laugh.

"You know what my favorite part is?" he said. "It spread because of reindeer. The migrations," he said. "In the summer, they went to the coast, and in the winter they moved inland. So you have all these Laplander nomads running around with their reindeer spreading this faith. Like a disease." From where she sat she could see out onto his back patio, where he and his friends had collected six or seven old toilets. They were supposed to be a postmodern commentary on the nature of patio furniture, but to her they looked like too many old toilets in a backyard.

"Yup," he said, "Geography is fate. I heard that somewhere." He typed, quickly. He looked up at her. "Heraclitus," he said.

"What?"

" 'Geography is fate,' " he said. "Heraclitus said it. The interwhatsits told me."

"Well," she said, "the knowledge of the interwhatsits is basically infinite."

"Basically the interwhatsits is God," he agreed.

"The interwhatsits forgives my sins," she said.

"Hey, good for you," he said, "making a joke about it."

That night, upstairs, drowsy from wine—his fingers clambering inarticulately for her bra—she thought about the bells. She wanted to hear them. She wanted to love him, she wanted to know perfectly and completely that this was perfect and complete.

"What if love is fate," she said. It felt like the first time she had told him she loved him, when she knew he would say it back.

"Listen," he said, "let's get a lease together."

"Of course," she said. Her heart skipped and skipped.

"You won't be in the church."

"I won't be in the church."

"We'll have a—loft apartment. With skylights."

"Skylights."

"Buttercup," he said.

"Matthew," she said.

The next morning she was making coffee in a French press and forgetting to stir the grounds. Matthew was making something he called morning delight. Like her mother, she cooked only when she had to, and he always cooked for them, spaghettis and curries and creative stews. From the garage she could hear his housemate's guitar, his morning attempt at dissonance.

"You know," he said, "today should really be the day. You can't save it for the end, because then you just have to go home. There could be some, you know, post-traumatic stress." He set a plate in front of her. The food was salty and fatty, eggs and potatoes and hot sauce. "This reminds me of fund-raising meals," she said. "Fund-raisers at church."

"Today," he said. He was cheerful, peppy, even. "Did you write it out," he said, "how you're going to say everything? How they'll react, what they might say, what you'll say in response?" It was something a therapist had told her to do. She hadn't done it.

She sighed.

"Tiina," he said.

She scraped her fork idly at the mash.

"Just three little words," he said. "That's it. Right?" He was talking through a mostly chewed mouthful. "Just say it. Say it right now." She took her plate to the sink and threw the food away in a compost bin. She rinsed her plate. The plate, she realized now, had the face of a fat Santa. " 'I don't believe.' Say it. Just think," he said, still cheerful, "what sky will fall?"

She walked out of the kitchen and through the sliding glass door. On the patio she sat down on one of the broken toilets. His housemate must have smoked out there sometimes, because there were cigarette butts inside all of the bowls, floating in old rain.

Matthew followed her. "You okay?" he said. He stood and looked at her in that careful way of his, like he was measuring something to the tenth of an inch. "I'm sorry," he said. "Say it's okay," he said. His voice was soft, like it was late at night, a

softness surreal in the bright sunlight, in the backyard of broken toilets.

"It's okay," she said, because that was what you said when
someone was sorry, in this other world of forgiveness.

He went back into the house, into the kitchen. He stood at
the counter and ate his morning delight from the pan.

She thought then about what Matthew had said, about just
doing things. People always said that things were easier said
than done, but that didn't make sense if the saying was the
doing; if, within the space of a few words, she was about to
swiftly and single-handedly dissolve the old and familiar bind-
ing of her family, irreparably and inconsolably. She thought
about her parents, if she knew them well enough to foresee
what their faces would do when they heard the news. She pic-
tured them laughing really hard, how her dad would wheeze,
his eyes teary, as if the laughter was too big for him. Her
mom's laugh was free and hearty, like all of her sisters', and so
infectious Tiina would run downstairs just to be a part of it.
But she couldn't picture them when she told them—would
her dad just withdraw, would he cry and shake and hold her
mom? What does the loss of a child look like on a face? How
is it shown?

But when she looked inside there was Matthew. He was sitting on the couch with his laptop. He winked. He looked too
skinny. He was too skinny. His skin was too white. In the light
he looked worse, and the light shone off his legs like off the
skin of a fish.

But when she looked down at her own legs, which were not
beautiful, lean gams but just sturdy things—and white, the
sun shining off them like off the skin of a fish—she wanted to
give him something to say thank you, for the plane ticket and

the patience and the years of watching her lie to her parents, as if he didn't exist at all.

She went inside and found her phone. She took it out onto the front steps, where it was warm, and where the sound of the guitar was muted. Like always, the phone rang and rang—as if there weren't people around—and just when she was sure no one would pick up, when her nervousness was becoming disappointment, her mother picked up.

"Tiina," she said, right away. Her voice was strained, excited. "Did you talk to Brita?"

"No," she said. "Why? What?" She felt shaky—she tried to remember how far along Brita was in her pregnancy—wasn't it too early? Was everything okay?

"Oh, I thought Brita might have called you, about Arnie. It's really just awful—no one can believe it."

"What," she said. "Arnie Aho?" Her hand rose suddenly to her chest—she thought of her cousin who'd fallen from a ladder into a window well. She thought of the Jankkila boy who'd shot his brother with a bow and arrow. "Well?" she said. "What?" In the background, she could hear her mom closing the living room doors, the sound of the little kids muted suddenly.

"Well," her mother said, her voice low now, "he—left Beth. He's gone. He left Beth with those kids. He put a note on the fridge about how he had all these doubts about the church. Well, of course everyone here is just in shock, and I guess Tim and Kathy are going to take the kids and Beth in for a while. I mean, everyone's just hoping, you know, that he'll come back— Hey, out, out," she said, her voice breaking off. There was the sound of the living room doors opening and closing again.

Tiina realized as she tried to say something that her hand was over her mouth. "Arnie Aho?" she said again, stupidly.

"He left this long note, but then Beth comes to find out he's really going to Hollywood. He has some plans of becoming an actor or something . . . so you know it was never really about the church, or anything, it's always the same thing, it's always something. Probably," she said, "probably there's a woman."

"Oh," Tiina said. She realized she was shaking somewhat. She kept seeing Beth, her curls falling into her purse. Her shoulders shaking. Tiina tried to picture Arnie, Arnie Aho, with his mustache, away in Hollywood with some woman.

Behind her the door opened, and Matthew came out and there was a wave of sound—the guitarist again—and then it quieted as the door closed.

"What's that?" her mother said.

"I'm outside." Tiina turned to look at him and shook her head, to wave him away.

Matthew sat down beside her. "Are you okay?" he said softly. She shook her head again.

"So!" her mother said.

"Well," Tiina said, "wow." She mouthed to Matthew that it was her mother.

"Anyway. That's the madness here," she said. "Paula's here. She's making them a casserole as we speak."

"Sure, of course."

"But how's the conference?" The memories of this lie waved over Tiina. The things she was supposed to come up with now, my God—she felt a flush of humiliation.

"It's good," she said feebly.

"Well, your dad and I are worried about you, you know."

"I know."

"Tiina—you know, we . . . we hope you're still confessing." She was talking more carefully now. "Even at the conference, even around all of those strangers," she said. "I know it's hard, and probably people are inviting you to do things that you don't feel comfortable doing, but you have to confess."

"I know," Tiina said. She was taking on a tone of annoyance, but it was partially with her mother and partially with Matthew. She started walking down the street. Matthew followed her, walking beside her. He took her hand.

"You can do it," he said quietly.

"So?" her mother said. "So tell me about the conference."

She shook her hand from Matthew's. They walked past an old man with a perfect halo of hair left, fastidiously at work on his hedges. Inside his house a phone rang and no one picked it up.

"Well," her mother said, her voice tense and quiet. "Would it help if—would you like to hear the Word?"

"Oh," she said, "sure," she said, and she would have held the phone away from her ear, but then Matthew would know something was wrong, so instead she had to press it even more tightly to her ear, and she tried not hear her mother—"Believe all of your sins and doubts forgiven"—the words slow and relished in her mouth, much too clear—"in Jesus's name and precious atoning blood," and she turned down another street, but there were only more people going about their daily lives. Matthew was still walking next to her. He was walking as if he was enjoying the walk, as if she were merely clarifying with a friend where they should meet up for dinner.

"Always, always believe. Always, always confess," her mother said. She was crying now in fat, mothering tears, her voice thick with relief. "I was so afraid to ask you," she said. "You know," she said, "sometimes with you I think of when you were little, there was a tornado, and I was rounding you all up in the basement, and I realized you weren't there, and I was running through the house, just screaming, Where's my Tiina? Where's my Tiina? and I finally found you, reading in the bathtub, and sometimes that's how I feel now, like you're just hiding away somewhere where you don't even want to be found." Tiina was circling the block, heading back toward Matthew's house. She didn't want to go there but she didn't know where else to go. She was outside, she was in another city, but she was trapped— she had no car, she had no keys, she had no way of going any- where. "And I just worry sometimes, I'm not a good enough mother—"

"Mom, don't say that," she said quietly.

"No, I know, I know what a poor example I am, and if I was braver I would ask you more, and I would ask about your school and your faith and I'm so afraid, it's just that I'm so afraid, I'm so poor, and I have to ask you, Tiina, can you forgive me for how poor a mother I've been? Can you find it in your heart"— she must have been wiping at her face with her sleeve—"can you find the grace to forgive even me?"

"Mom," she said, her voice gentle now, "of course." She felt her pulse rise, sick and thready, and she couldn't believe she had to say it. She thought of everything she could say instead—I don't want to have this conversation right now, for instance. She thought about Matthew, she thought about the sun-filled apartment they were going to have, but she had been trained too long and too hard, and instead she stopped in the middle of the sidewalk and kept her back to him and said, quickly, so the words could be gotten out of her, "Believe all of your sins forgiven in Jesus's name and precious blood," skipping the extra bits about doubt, and she did not look at Matthew and she did not look at the stranger driving down the street and she waited, Henny Penny–like, for the sky to fall, but no matter what, it did not fall and it did not fall, and instead there was only Matthew and his housemate's guitar and her mother on the phone, and no matter what none of it went away at all.

"I'm sorry," she said when she hung up. She turned around, and he was standing there. He didn't hug her and he walked away. The rest of the night they carefully avoided each other. He made dinner and they ate it together, quietly, until at last he said, in between bites, "You know, the best thing about the church is your family, and the worst thing about your family is the church," to which she said nothing at all, because it was true, and she hated that he knew her better than she knew herself. It was only before they fell asleep that he said, putting his hand in hers, "This is my favorite part of the day," like he always did, which was his own kind of forgiveness, and it was only then that she slept, her body crouched inside his, his easy sleep, her uneasy dreams.

The night she cheated on Matthew she had been an unbeliever for almost two years. When the new man rolled from her— James, who only liked reading things that were true—she watched the fan go about and about on the ceiling, and she thought about how she was supposed to want to cling to him but she only wanted him to leave. He was better looking and a better kisser but the sex had been the same, the same sudden stop, the same awkwardness of not having gotten what she had bargained for, what she had paid for.

Finally she rose and went into the shower, and she lay down flat, hating the way thighs look bigger flat, washing away his semen, and she had the concrete thought that she had become officially a sinner—she was no good in both the church's world and in the world she had chosen; to all eyes she had sinned. She was freed from nothing, liberated from nothing. It wasn't about the sinning at all, it was what you did about the sinning, and she had no means of forgiveness about her, and she thought suddenly of Arnie Aho, and she wondered where he was, if he was living off this woman's money, or maybe he had become a truck driver and listened to Stephen Kings a country long. She wondered if he had shaved his mustache, if now his upper lip hung impotent and white. She wanted to call him, to see if he was okay, if he'd gotten what he wanted from this life, and she had the half thought that she would go and find the church phone book, but she realized that she wasn't in the phone book anymore and neither was he and anyway there was no phone book for those who had left.

And she thought about the cat, sleeping inside the vinyl cello case, watching her mother cry when she told her she was leaving the church, that she had left. Her mother had been so content, she had been talking about things they got wrong in Iraq and how to show love to your students, which to her was exactly the same conversation, and then Tiina just destroyed it all, and the cat went back to sleep in the vinyl cello case. She thought then that she had freed herself of the fear of leaving only for Matthew, that she had finally proved to herself that she was leaving for herself. She had decided that there simply wasn't any such thing as sinning anymore, because it seemed so obvious that green nails weren't a sin, and if they were wrong about that they were probably wrong about everything, and the cat held all the hope for her, the cat she didn't like and who had a stupid name, and who could sleep through even this. But in the shower she looked at her nails and she realized they weren't green and in fact she never painted them green, or red, or anything, like the way she had pierced her ears but she never wore earrings, and every time she wanted to she had to repunch the hole, and she'd feel sick, feeling the skin not want to give but making it give.

She sat in that shower until James came and knocked on the door. "You okay in there?" he said.

"Just relaxing," she said, and she realized she was still a liar. Me and Arnie, she thought, we sinners, we are just lying to ourselves, we are just alone.

# THE SUN AND THE SOW

THE WAITRESSING WAS supposed to have lasted just the summer, but it had been a year and Paula was still at the nursing home. She was still being yelled at by the old lady who was a Holocaust survivor, and she was still being yelled at by her supervisor, for having been yelled at by a Holocaust survivor, since there were only three left at the Jewish Community Center, and since the center, whatever else it did, prided itself on keeping the survivors alive. "Everyone else knows to pour the boiling water over the tea bag," Miriam snapped at her, "everyone else. You're the only one who pours the water in first. The only one."

"Pull your shit together," Manny said to her, back in the kitchen. She knew she should have minded, but even when Manny yelled at her she didn't really mind—he had such beautiful eyes, with eyelashes too heavy for his eyelids, like a doll.

The old Russian ladies who made the food laughed at her. "You should put some makeup on," they said to her in the kitchen, pinching her cheek with a gloved hand. "You should do your hair. Then maybe he sees you staring at him." But when she ironed the white collared shirt, or when her sisters did her hair in a fancy bun, they would laugh harder. "Look who thinks she's so pretty now!"

The old men liked her, though. She was a natural blonde, straight to the roots. "You should be in a movie," they would say. "Eh? Eh?" They winked. She would blush, and half the table would clap. But then they would realize she hadn't put lemon in their water, and they'd send her off to the kitchen. Sometimes she just never came back with the lemon, because she knew they would forget. For her favorites, though, for Irene, for Otto, she always remembered, even if they forgot, even if Irene didn't realize she always put ice in her milk, even if Otto was too tired to see she had put his dressing on the side. Otto never said she should be in movies; he only said, sometimes, slipping her a sweaty one-dollar bill, "You got hair like the sun." She had hair like the sun but a face like a sow. Her grandmother had said it herself, maybe because it was, after all, her grandmother's face.

But like her grandmother, she was strong. She wanted to cry sometimes, but she never did. She could tell other people thought she ought to be crying, because they would comfort her. After Miriam had yelled at her about the tea, Irene took her hand. Irene's hand was the softest hand she had ever touched.

"Don't worry, I'll quit," Paula said.

"Don't quit on us," Irene said. "What'll I do? What'll you do?"

"Move."

"Where are you going to go?"

"Minnesota, maybe," Paula said.

"Listen," Irene said, "you have a family who loves you. Family is all that matters. I've lived in three countries and eighteen cities and I've got a collection of golf pencils to prove it and let me tell you, it's never the place, it's the people. Your family loves you?" Irene said.

Paula nodded.

"Of course they do," Irene said, "of course they do." She nodded her head. "Come here," she said, and when Paula leaned in Irene said, not really whispering, "My daughter-in-law looks like a whore."

"Oh," Paula said.

"Don't tell her," Irene said. She let go of Paula's hand.

"No, never," Paula said.

"You going to go after that pretty boy, the pretty boy in the kitchen?" Irene asked. She was trying to say it quietly but she couldn't say anything quietly anymore, and the whole table turned. It reminded Paula of her uncle's farm, of the cows on the hill when the milk truck came by, like all the heads turned on the same neck.

At home it seemed to Paula as if the JCC did not exist. She had taken over her brothers' old room, the Fortress of Solitude, and for the first time she was sleeping alone. She liked it, mostly. She had Tiina's old laptop, which only worked when it was plugged in. She had a snowboard she should have sold. On the wall she had put up her pictures and at some point she had realized they were all of her family and that none of her school friends had made it up there, but she never did anything to change that. Maybe it was because she felt so bad about still living in her parents' basement, taking the occasional community college class, soaking up her parents' money when they had five more kids to send to school and they couldn't take out any more loans. Maybe she just felt bad about being the ordinary one. She couldn't even play the piano very well. At least she could sing, though. At least community college was cheap. "Cash is king," her dad said. "Be useful," her mom said.

She'd written her mom's saying on a notecard and put it on her bulletin board. Next to the note was a card that read, "Friends are like stars. Even if you don't see them, you know they're always there." It was from a friend she never saw. Surrounding the note were collections of wedding announcements and baby announcements from church. The brides were all too young, but she envied them anyway. She envied that they knew they were wanted, their hair in too-tight curls, their breasts both hidden and displayed by stiff white cloth. What was that like, she wondered, to know you were wanted, not because of everything you did, not because of everything you gave?

The next day was one of the good days and someone nearly died and the EMTs from the hospital across the road had to come. It was smart, she realized, to have built the senior center across from the hospital. She would never have thought of that. And when the EMTs arrived it was better still because they had to give oxygen, and everything was in chaos. "I think he needs oxygen," she said, and the EMT looked up and said, "You're right," surprised. The EMT was cute, even if his hair was too short and too gelled, as if saving lives was like surfing.

Best was that Manny got all out of sorts. His rule over the center was threatened and he tried to give directions—"You can take him into the visiting area," he said, but the EMTs just ignored him. "Uh-uh," they said, "it's best in these situations not to move people."

"Paula, I'm counting on you for room trays," he said then, to restore his order. She walked away smiling, even though room trays were the worst duty, which was why he had to count on her. It sounded like such a basic task but pushing the carts was never easy, the gravy always tipped, and it was depressing;

the food never masked the other smells. And there was the resident who stared straight ahead and didn't acknowledge that you were alive.

The ones with Alzheimer's were worst, of course. It always reminded her of Grandma. Grandma had had Alzheimer's, and Aunt Marijo probably did, too. Aunt Marijo always tried to feed them three and four lunches when they came to visit now. She would look at all the cleaned-off dishes in the sink and say, "My word, and I thought I did dishes last night."

But Grandma stole things. Once, Paula's doll. It was the only doll she cared about—the American Girl doll you got when you turned eight because the catalog recommended it for girls ages eight and up. Her sisters still had theirs. Paula's had been Samantha, because Samantha had the nicest clothes—red velvets, plaids, lace collars, Mary Janes. In the magazines Samantha had tea sets, and her wardrobe was lined with velour, and the wicker of the outdoor patio set curved and bent more beautifully than anything Paula had ever seen in real life. "That's so Samantha of you," Tiina would say when Paula touched a particularly smooth silk dress at the mall.

It's just nice, she wanted to say.

But she was a server at the JCC's Senior Living Center, and her job was to wear white on top and black on the bottom, and black tennis shoes that would not scuff the floor. And to keep her hair out of her face and out of the food, since, as Manny pointed out, she was the only blonde in the place and they would know who'd done it.

That night, before she fell asleep, she let herself pretend. She would be in the kitchen, chopping something. Carrots. She would be using the dairy knife since it was a dairy day, she would not be making that mistake. And Manny would need something—he would need the knife. "Can I borrow that," he would say, leaning over. When he leaned over she would smell his cologne. And when she handed him the knife he would clasp his hand over hers. "Say," he would ask, "have you always worked here?" But the joke would be friendly. And he would take his hand and brush a fallen strand of hair back behind her ear.

It was Otto who almost talked her into asking Manny out. "Listen, sunshine," Otto said, "someday someone's going to realize what you got. You just keep doing what you're doing," he said. "Someone's going to appreciate you."

Then he had started to choke on the soup, and the matzoh balls fell into his lap like something from inside his lungs. When she was helping him clean up, he said, "Life is too short to eat bad matzoh ball soup."

Okay, she'd thought, in the kitchen. Life is too short to eat bad matzoh ball soup. She wished there was a magnet for that. Afterward she had stood in the kitchen and studied Manny's back. He was magnetic, that was the word. He was the kind of person who walked down the street and you didn't want to like him but you had to. You wanted to be close to him, for the same reason you went to museums or sat on beaches, simply to be done staring at the ugly things, to put them from your mind for an afternoon or an evening. It was why no one had crushes on her. She was the reminder of how hard the world was; it was in her face, the unfairness of life.

But still, Otto had said that someday someone would appreciate her. She thought maybe it was true. Maybe there was another Otto out there. Probably the Otto wasn't Manny, though, she thought, and turned away, back to stacking the room trays, hot and dry now from the washer.

At her parents' house she told Julia and Leena and Anni and Uppu about Manny. The girls would come down to her room and sit on the couch she had rescued from the side of the road. The Fortress was always freezing, because of the air vent, and they pulled blankets up to their necks and drank Diet Coke she kept on the basement windowsill to keep it cool.

"He always washes his car," Paula told them. "He got a tattoo," she told them.

"Tiina's always talking about getting a tattoo," Julia said. "She's so impulsive like that. It's kind of immature."

"She better not," Anni said. "Mom will lock herself in the bedroom and not come out again."

"I would get one," Leena said. "You know, if I left."

"Really?" Julia said.

"Manny's is a bulldog," Paula said, almost proudly. She didn't tell them about how when he got it done it was covered in cellophane and the cellophane was stuck on with masking tape and she kept hoping it would fall off and she would have to help him press it back on.

But the next week his ex-girlfriend showed up. She looked like Irene's daughter-in-law: they both wore tight pants and stilettos, as if the nursing home was a shopping mall and they had to look hot, hot, hot. They did look hot, hot, hot. Manny's ex-girlfriend's hair was black and glossed and she straightened it between her fingers, constantly. Manny disappeared out in the parking lot with her and it was an hour before he came back in. He put his hand on her shoulder. "Paula," he said, "never tell someone you love them too soon. Take it from me."

"Okay," she said.

"Promise me."

"Okay," she said. She thought, I love you, Manny.

When she went home, Brita and her boys were all visiting and she told Brita the story. Brita had four boys and she wanted her siblings to get married and have kids too, even Tiina, and she thought it was a little immature of Paula to go moping after some guy she couldn't date. "How come Nels is the only other one to get married?" Brita said. "How come you can't just date one of those Finn boys in town?"

But Paula knew Brita was wrong about the Finn boys. They were never going to date her. And she knew Brita was wrong about Manny. For instance, Brita thought it was the girlfriend who had talked about love too soon but the way Manny had looked, as if there was something he was trying to forget, made Paula think it was Manny. She understood him. It was why he said things to her, things like not to go downstairs because they were hot-boxing the janitor's closet, things like how his brother was paralyzed from diving off a cliff and now Manny noticed every building that didn't have ramps.

"Listen," Julia said, "he's just using you because you're too nice. Just quit already and go to school full-time. Do social work like you always say you want to do. Get your own place." Julia always talked to her like that, like she was older than Paula. All of these things were true, but Paula had never even liked school. And she liked the Fortress of Solitude. She liked not paying rent. She liked living where there was always the sound of people walking above her head. And there was Manny. There was Irene, and Otto.

Sometimes she wondered about Otto. Some of the residents said he wasn't a real Holocaust survivor. He didn't have numbers on his arm. He said he'd been in the camps, though, he swore it. Each time, though, he named a different camp.

Miriam muttered under her breath about him. One day she spat on the floor. Paula skipped the lemon for her water. After all, who knew what was true anymore? Who knew who had been where? But then she felt guilty. She hadn't been in the Holocaust, and she wasn't even Jewish. She brought Miriam her lemon and apologized for the delay.

"What?" Miriam said.

"Just your lemon," Paula said. She set it carefully atop the glass.

Miriam reminded her of her grandma more than anyone else. She was unexpectedly mean, like Grandma had been. Like Grandma, she told good stories, but hers were sadder.

"When they came for us," Miriam had said, "the last thing I had eaten was a piece of cake."

Friday night she drove to her parents' house after Shabbat, as usual, and she saw Brita's van, as usual, but inside everyone was sitting on the couches, silent. No one looked at her when she came in.

"What?" she said. Maybe because she worked in a place of death, she thought someone was dead. She thought of everyone who wasn't sitting there right now: Tiina in New York, Nels in Minneapolis, Simon in Boston. She almost began to cry. No one said anything. "What?" she said.

Her mother looked at Leena, pointedly. Leena was eighteen and normally looked sixteen, and right now she looked even younger, with her eyes all baggy from crying.

"I'm pregnant," Leena said. The way she was sitting, her knees pulled into her chest, Paula could not even look at her belly, to see if she had missed something.

"With who?" Paula said, and realized the question did not make sense. She felt a shock so severe—she felt like she had been a fool. The world was never what she had thought it was.

She was naive; here she had thought Leena was like her, one of the quiet ones, one of the good ones. We were in this together, she wanted to say.

Leena did not look up.

"She isn't telling," her mom said, sighing. "Apparently she thinks it's okay to just run off with whomever, like it doesn't matter—"

"That's enough," her dad said.

"The Wisuri girl is pregnant," Uppu said.

"I said that's enough," her dad interrupted.

They were all quiet.

It was a silent night. They ate in silence. Her parents took Leena upstairs into their bedroom, and from the basement vent Paula could hear them trying to talk to Leena but she couldn't make out what they were saying. Julia and Anni and Uppu sat with her and they went through the options endlessly but none of them even knew she had been sleeping with somebody.

"She should have used protection," Julia said, and Anni and Uppu blushed. "I feel like she did it just because she was so relieved to have someone like her."

"Just because boys always chase you," Julia said.

"They do not," Julia said, but it was clear she was pleased. Julia thrived on being the pretty one, with her unearthly white hair and green eyes. Paula was tired—her eyes kept closing on her—but she waited until she heard Leena come out of their parents' bedroom, and then she went upstairs and into Leena and Anni's room. It was always strange being in her old room, seeing the places her things used to be.

"Leena," she said, "you can tell me."

"It's not anyone's business," Leena said. And she began to cry. "I'm fine," she said. "It's all fine. I'm stupid."

"Who was it?" Paula said. "Just tell me. I'm your sister. You can tell me."

"It doesn't matter," Leena said. "He doesn't live here. He'll never live here. It was all—everything was an accident. I was stupid and wrong. There's nothing else to say."

Paula reached out to hug Leena, but Leena moved away.

"Please," Paula said.

"Why does it matter anyway?" Leena said. "I'm not going to marry him and he's not going to marry me and this baby is just going to have one lonely, pathetic mother."

"Don't say that," Paula said, but she couldn't have agreed more.

Because Paula could not tell anyone at church—the news would spread, she was sure, in a day, but in the meantime they would all behave like it was not happening—she told Irene. "My sister is a teenager and pregnant," Paula said.

"I was a teenager and pregnant," Irene said.

"You were?"

"Well," Irene said, "I got married. I had my baby. Now he's marrying a girl who looks like a whore."

Then the alarm on the doors to the parking lot went off. "Paula," Manny yelled from down the hall, and Paula guessed that Otto had escaped. Paula was the only one who could talk him back in, because she knew to tell him the Holocaust was over. Running out of the room she saw the clock, the large analog numbers, and she knew it would be nine or nine-thirty by the time she left and yet she knew she would only be paid until eight-thirty; they always did that. Julia always said she should sue, but she was the one who would be sued—for being slow, for spilling soup. You couldn't sue the entire Jewish Community Center for a half hour of pay. You couldn't sue a place with people who had survived the Holocaust.

Out in the cold, looking for Otto between the rows of cars, she thought about Leena, how people would look at her in the grocery store, with her ringless finger. She put her hand on her stomach and felt the muscles move as she ran. She wondered about her own children. Would they have faces like a sow? "Listen," she would tell them. "Once, I kissed a beautiful man. His name was Manny. He wore cologne. When he walked in the room, everyone turned to look at him. And he kissed me." She would tell the story about the knife, about cutting carrots. Her youngest daughter, whose middle name would be Paula, after her, would watch her, wide-eyed. She would touch her daughter's cheek with her incredibly soft hand. "Come here," she would say, and her daughter would lean in close. "All of my children are beautiful," she would say. "Just kiss the boy."

## TOTAL LOSS

RIGHT BEFORE THEY had sex and only right before they had sex Julia felt something was possible between them. But Will was like that, or their sex was like that—kept forever at bay and then, once held up close, revealed to be much further away than before. She was compulsively desiring of him until she had him, and then she was ashamed to see that having him was not enough, and this deepened the distance yet again. But she could not quit, halving herself and doubling her wants until there was hardly anything left of her to sustain. It was New Year's Eve and especially tonight she wanted to be hopeful, but instead the holiday had given the sex a special artificiality and she regretted everything, and afterward she continued drinking, willing herself into drunkenness until she went to bed and coached herself to pass out.

If she could have she would have slept until it was late in the day, but her dreams were thin and anxious, and interrupted at their breaking point by the sound of the phone ringing close to her ear.

"Where's your violin?" her mother snapped.

"What time is it?"

"The house is burning down, we need to know if it's in the house, where is it?"

She sat up in bed, but Will turned over and slept more tightly. She forced herself to think about the question of the violin.

"It's at home," she said. "Here, it's here." The answer was complicated by her being in Will's apartment, and not her own.

"I have to call Simon," her mother said, "we can't find his viola, either," and she hung up, leaving Julia again in the emptiness of Will's sleeping body. She knew she would not fall back asleep, and she called her dad's phone to get the actual story. He spoke so slowly and quietly he seemed to be mimicking the hundreds of miles between Julia and her childhood home, as if the words took longer because of distance. His thoughts wandered. The house would be fine, except the bedroom. Well, not fine, he said. Well, the floor might cave. He told her the story of everyone escaping. There was the sound of firemen calling to one another calmly.

When the call was over she lay back down. She pretended to sleep, going so far as to breathe deeply and evenly. When Will woke she rolled slowly over, as if from heavy slumber. She watched him select a T-shirt from a hanger. She had the sense even in this ordinary action of how extraordinary he was; Will existed for her in a permanent state of—she didn't want to think it, but the word was exotic—of exotic good looks. He had the dramatic features of high-end ads, and even in cotton drawstring pajamas seemed to be selling something. Will was the first person she had dated to not tell her on a regular basis that she was beautiful. Her last boyfriend had called her a snow queen; the one before that, a princess of the elves. Her boyfriends let her hair—white, like hundreds of Finns she knew—hang loose over their faces, over their chests. Will was unimpressed by everything, and this impressed her. He was older than her by five years and he made her feel old, and mature—even the distance of his interest in her made her feel old. I'm having a casual relationship, she told herself, and I'm fine.

"That was my mom," she said, as she followed him to the kitchen. "On the phone last night."

"Yeah?" he said.

"There was a fire," she said. "An old outlet set a mattress on fire, I guess." She looked to see if he was listening. "But everyone's okay."

"That's good," he said absently. He stared at his computer. He was often like this—he reacted to all her allusions to her eight siblings, her religious apostasy, her mother's antics with equal aloofness. To him her past was utterly surmountable, perhaps because of his own, what with his inner-city stories, his friend shot, his scars from bar fights. She liked it—she had always wanted a man who had also lived through something— and she wanted to emulate this same boredom with drama, to be reticent and hermetic like him, seemingly unfettered by the past.

She thought about telling him the rest of the story: her mom discovering the mattress aflame, running down to the basement to wake up Brita and her husband and their kids, swaddling the baby in a nearby sleeping bag, running out into the snow in bare feet—how lucky that Anni and Uppu weren't in their room but in Minnesota for the holiday.

"My home," she said, more to herself.

"Yeah, I lost mine years ago," he said. "Fire would have been an improvement, come to think of it."

"Yeah?"

"Long story," he said, but he clearly wasn't going to tell it.

"I might go help out." She said this as it occurred to her. Mostly she wanted to see if he would want her to stay.

"Yeah," he said.

"For a couple of weeks."

"It'll be good for you—it won't be that bad." He stared at the screen and she went to her computer, and they sat in near silence. He liked to spend the morning reading the news. He said if he wanted his students to care about the world, he had to care about the world. He was a history teacher, like Nels, and he did everything in the name of his students, like her mother. He didn't find these connections interesting. The sun moved threateningly slow across the cramped counter. He didn't like to be disturbed, and she didn't like to disturb him.

At lunch she faked that she had bought a ticket, to see what he would say.

"Do you want a ride to the airport? When's the flight?"

So she bought one. She was just working at a lingerie store anyway, waiting for a real job to come through. She had applications everywhere, at nonprofits, at research groups, at public relations firms, but she knew it hurt her that she had gone to a state school, even if her grades were good, even if her professors had liked her. She knew she surprised people—they didn't expect her to be smart. But in the meantime she was tired of holding a tape measure. She was tired of feeling the sweat and heat of women's armpits as she measured someone else's chest. Her feet hurt from standing, and by the end of the day her face felt strangely chalky from makeup. She had hoped this would make her boss fire her, but her boss was too desperate for help, and even acted sympathetic.

"I'm coming home," she said to her mom, and her mom began to cry, she was so happy.

"It's just a visit," she said.

"I know," her mom said. "I'm just so happy when my kids come home."

When Will dropped her off at the airport—kissing her briefly good-bye—she grabbed her suitcase from the backseat on her own. She walked away from him briskly and did not look back. It was a limited, gendered power, the power of removal, but she tried to exercise it when she could, to at least prove to herself that she was capable of walking away.

Her mother picked her up a half hour late.

"Just wait until you see it," her mother clucked in the car. "You'll never believe it." Julia thought she was talking about the burnt house, but she was talking about the new house the insurance company had found for them while the second floor was being rebuilt. In the only example of divine insurance justice Julia could think of, their policy had stated that the insurance company had to move them to a house that was nearby, of comparable value, and could accommodate a similar number of people. Her family, with their nine children, had spent the past twenty years rearranging the four-bedroom house to sleep twelve (Brita and her husband and their boys had recently moved in), and so the insurance company had had to move them into what was literally a mansion.

It took a full fifteen minutes to tour the mansion, to inspect its seven bedrooms, its wine cellar (already being used for the cat's litter box), its varied cornices and closets, its not one but two sunrooms. The overall effect was of newness, openness, like a hangar wing for miniature aircraft, with the occasional capitulation to humans—a stainless steel stove and glass coffee tables and everywhere the sinking sensation of carpet. It was so absurd—a house that finally fit their family, but too late, and its luxury only borrowed.

Julia found Brita in the second sunroom, trying to nurse her baby.

"Howdy," Julia said shyly.

"I have no milk," Brita said. "Do you know what that's like, when you can't nurse your own baby?" She switched Nick from one breast to the other, and Julia saw for an instant the frank brown of her nipples, swollen and wide. She tried not to stare.

Though no one said it—and it made sense not to say it—it was clear a truce had fallen, wherein no one was to directly confront the fact that now that Julia had left the church the past summer, three of the nine of them had left the church. Julia charted how closely conversation would come to mentioning the uncomfortable fact but never quite touch it—how her mom would ask if everyone had heard about how the Niskanen boy had lost his faith and then, adroitly, Brita would say that Makelas had invited everyone over for coffee lunch. It was a game in which the rules were never expressed and yet were very clear to all the players.

In a way, Julia was grateful for the game. She had always been the peacemaking middle child, calming Brita or Tiina down, and even when she had left the church there had been no dramatic tears, like with Tiina, no banging doors, like with Simon; she had just announced it before she had moved to New York, telling them at the same time that she had found a job and that she did not believe, and then she had gone to her room and pretended to read a book, her hands shaking so that the type was illegible. And since then she had tried to seem like an approvable daughter—she never mentioned who she was dating, or made references to drinking or movies, and she took off her nail polish and makeup when she went home, and kept her shirts long and loose. She wore bras that shrank her chest. She looked clean and wholesome and decidedly not herself.

But these concessions were preventative rather than reparative. She spoke to Brita now only when her babies were born, or around other big news, and already there was the uncomfortable trend of the three unbelieving siblings talking to one another more frequently than they talked to the believing siblings, and vice versa. When she came home she still felt close to Anni and Uppu, because they were only in high school and had not yet decided to go or stay, but even in their interactions she felt the future hanging between them, and she was cautious. She wanted to prove that she could leave the church and not become a disaster, that she could still be a good sister, a good aunt, find a good husband—she could still be loved, just the same. At night when she got in bed next to Anni she wanted to ask, "I seem happy, right?" but it was the kind of question that, in being asked, answered itself, and instead she rolled in close to Anni and slept more cleanly than she could remember, the old childhood security of many people asleep in one place, the uncomplicated comfort of someone in her bed who was not her lover, and even when their mother appeared at the door, waking them up for church, she didn't mind.

She dressed with Anni, rooting through their suitcases for tights without holes, and went to the church she had always gone to, sitting in the back pew with Anni and Uppu like she always had, everything seemingly the same but of course impossibly different. People studied her, looking for signs of difference.

Welcome, people said, and she blushed each time they did not say God's Peace to her, but it had to be borne—she had to show the little girls that these things did not affect her.

By the time they got back to the mansion she felt calmer—they were just a family again. There was Anni on the piano and her dad closing his eyes, upright in a chair. Paula was making lunch, meat and potatoes. Leena had come over so her boy could play with Brita's boys—they were always together now, the two mothers—and they sat at the kitchen table and criticized all the new baby names in the church newsletter. "More fake-sounding last names for first names," Brita announced. Brita's baby cried from the car seat, and her mother picked him up and impatiently murmured to him as they had all been sung to, patting his back, It's o-kay, she sang, it's o-kay, it's o-kay, my ba-by.

The baby rubbed his eyes with his hands and she saw, for an uncomfortable instant, a vision of Will. It was something he did, and the gesture was always bizarrely infantile and she would recognize for an instant that he was only human.

In her mother's arms Nick quieted. How do I have this, Julia wondered, how does this work, how will I be happy the rest of my life?


The old house looked worse than she'd imagined. From the street it looked like a kicked-in sand castle, with the extra abandonment that came from the care of boarded windows. Inside the house the upstairs walls had a patina of soot and Anni and Uppu's bedroom itself was a cave of melted things—mirrors, and doll hair, the old Christmas dresses in a waxen heap from the collapse of the hangers, everything destroyed just enough to still be recognizable.

The entire house, it turned out, had to be emptied. Everything that could be used again—that was not a toiletry, that was not food, that was not perishable, that was not actually burned—had to be cleaned, and boxed, and put into storage until the house was rebuilt. Everything burned had to be inventoried, its original price accounted for, its depreciation calculated. The insurance called it accounting for "total loss." Technically speaking, the insurance would pay someone else to do it, but if you did it yourself they paid you instead, and her parents had inherited the working-class attitude of refusing to pay someone to do anything they thought they could do themselves. Instead, they wore masks and for hours they packed boxes—first the boxes had to be built—and Julia's shoulders hurt and her thighs hurt and every time she walked a box outside the cold air made her taste blood in her throat but she kept doing it because it had to be done.

Occasionally someone went to a gas station and brought back Diet Coke and they sat on boxes and opened up cans. "What a lot of junk," her dad said. He was embarrassed by it all, by the dumpster outside, slowly filling with Grandma's broken chairs, the 1940s *Life* magazines no one had sold, the violin bows that had warped and never been rehaired, dead Christmas lights, the still-standing tree. As they opened each drawer, his irritation increased. "What is this doing here?" he would ask, as if realizing for the first time that he'd lived in a house where a withered orange peel sat alongside a staling swimsuit in the same drawer as the old church songbooks.

Simon called her from Boston. "You have to keep an eye out for my stuff," he said. "Don't let them touch it. Don't even look at it."

"I wouldn't," she said, slightly annoyed.

"Just throw away any journals. Basically, if it has my name

on it, throw it away. No, hide it away somewhere so I can go through it later."

"Okay," she said. Paula and Anni and Uppu walked back and forth from the house to the dumpster, still carrying boxes.

"Wouldn't it be great if Dad found some of my gay porn?" Simon said.

"Not really."

"Better yet," Simon said, "pictures of Christopher. Hey, should we plant some? Hey, you want to plant some?"

"No."

"It would just be, like, Dad thinks he's packing away books in the boys' room and then—boom. Boom." He laughed and she joined the laughter halfheartedly. "So," Simon said, "anyone asked whether Will exists yet?"

"No," she said. She had an image of Will, sitting on the bed. She was lotioning his back. She saw the narrowness of his waist.

"Not going to tell them, huh."

"No."

"I told them about Christopher."

"I shouldn't have told you," she said. She sighed. Also, she wanted to say, Will isn't the kind of boyfriend you admit to, someone who isn't going to marry you and doesn't want to meet your parents. At least Christopher had come to Christmas once—quiet, sweet Christopher, bringing everyone fancy gift baskets—even if he had never come again.

"They can compromise too, you know," he said. "You have to be uncomfortable in their world, they can be uncomfortable in yours."

"Yeah," she said, to make him stop talking about it, but she didn't agree. She was more pragmatic than Simon and Tiina. She didn't believe honesty was really the best policy.

By the end of the day it hurt to sit down, to stand up again. She went out and picked up takeout from an Indian place.

"What is this?" her dad said.

"So it was nice of your work to give you time off," her mom said.

"Yeah," she said. They were under the impression that she worked for a lingerie company at a corporate level. She let this impression stick around.

"What do you do all day anyway?" Brita said.

"I don't want to come home to talk about work," Julia said. "I came home to not talk about work."

"Why can't you just work here?" her mom said. "What, we don't have those kinds of jobs here?"

"Mom," Julia said.

"Then what," Brita said. "You're too good for us now."

"No."

"Everything we have, New York can do better."

"Can we just eat this?" her dad said.

After dinner she called Will, to prove to herself he existed.

"Hey, sweetie," he said. She hated how this always worked, the sweetie stuff. It wasn't supposed to work. She was supposed to be resistant to it, but instantly she felt happier. She told him about Simon, his joke about the porn.

He laughed, and she felt better. "So how are you doing, what have you been up to?" she said idly. She paced the bedroom she was sharing with Anni. She went through Anni's stash of jewelry.

"Actually, I had a shit day."

"What happened? Something with your students? Was it Tito again?"

"I don't really want to go into it." He had a nervous laugh, and he emitted it now.

"Oh, sure," she said, but really she resented it, everything she didn't know and would never know. They talked of other things, then. Nothing things. She was appalled to discover herself talking about the weather and carrying boxes in the cold. She was a bore to herself, but when she talked to him she became too nervous to say all of the interesting things. "Okay," she said, finally, moodily.

"Okay what?"

"No, nothing. Never mind."

"Hey, I'm listening," he said, his voice soft now.

"I just—I want to know what's going on with you. I'm calmer when I know what's up with you."

"Uh," he said, "that's weird. You really feel anxious? Really?"

"Well, I didn't mean it like that," she said. They talked more and he was at least aware enough to try to fix it, but she had said it, and it was too late.


Four full days of packing later, they had made it to the upstairs rooms. Julia was valiantly tackling the basement all on her own, even though she realized she was tiring herself out on purpose. Mostly she was succeeding. Occasionally memories came to her—the wind tunnels beneath the bridge—and she would divert her mind away and go back to work. Only sometimes she faltered, and let herself see a night more fully, the memory of being lifted, and then she would wince in recalling it, how he was too smooth, the ugliness behind his suaveness in its implication of practice. But it was true that the intensity of the memories was fading. The demands of her family washed New York to the opacity of early strokes of watercolor, hardly there.

That night, trying to warm the blankets, Anni said, "When are you leaving?"

"I don't know—when should I leave?" She was supposed to be back by the beginning of the following week, but she felt inclined to stay—or, rather, neither choice was preferable.

"I just want everyone home," Anni said.

"Me, too," Julia said automatically. She considered whether this was true.

"Julia," she said, "do you think you'll ever come back?"

"Never say never," Julia said, because it seemed kind, but she thought, never. It was not the kind of thing you could go back on, she reflected. Now that she had seen the world, now that she had been in it—she could not go back. She tried to imagine it, for a minute, being like Brita or Nels, accepting life where you had babies and had babies, where she would have to marry some carpenter from Minnesota. Never, she thought, and she thought of Will, his apartment with exposed brick walls—small, yes, but his, and the place quiet and clean. The two futures were so dissimilar she was sure they did not exist on the same continent.

It was near midnight and the house was asleep except for Anni and Uppu, up doing homework. Julia put a movie on her laptop, a romantic comedy, because even if she knew better she liked the inevitability, knowing from the outset who would stick with whom, the comfort of narrative. The movie was almost over when Anni came into the room. Julia pushed the headphones down to her neck.

"I know what you're doing," Anni said, and rolled her eyes.

"Sorry," Julia said quietly.

"What is it?"

"Something with a happy ending, you know," she said, and Anni climbed into bed next to her. She started the movie again, and took out the headphones and turned down the volume, quiet but loud enough so they could both hear. They were still watching, wholly absorbed—Julia had long recognized the way people in her family stared at televisions, like third-world refugees—when Brita walked in, Nick on her hip.

Julia shut the laptop. Anni jerked up. Brita turned around as hard as she could, banging the door behind her.

"Shit," Anni said, "shit," and Julia saw that her face was red. Poor Anni, she thought, feeling sorry for her—Anni had always been stuck being the good church girl, the one whose job it was to not create a fuss, to the point that Anni had never gotten very much attention, had always floated by in the background of everyone's attention.

Julia went to look for Brita, who was standing in the giant kitchen, looking out the big bay window, bouncing the wailing Nick.

"Listen," Julia said, "that had nothing to do with her. She was being totally good about it. I just want you to know. Here, I'll take him, you go make him a bottle." She took Nick, and his body stiffened angrily. She patted his back. Brita turned on the faucet, waiting for the water to get warm.

"Why do you have to do that?" Brita asked.

"Do what?" Bouncing Nick was tiring, but he was quiet now.

"Why'd you let Anni," she said. She scooped the formula and shook the bottle.

"I mean, she's not a little kid anymore, Brita, I don't know—"

"I mean, I expect that from Tiina—Tiina would do that. But you, I mean—" She took Nick from Julia, gave him the bottle.

"Me what?"

"You—you didn't use to be like this, Julia. You used to be— you used to be—"

"What?"

"You don't do things like Tiina, right? You don't, like, drink and stuff? I mean, you've always been—you were always good. Tiina was always in trouble, she was always sneaking out, but you were good. You were good in high school. I made you Paulie's godmother, once upon a time."

"I'm still Paulie's godmother," Julia said, but it stung.

"What happened?"

"Nothing happened. I don't believe anymore."

"Why not? Why can't you?"

"I don't know." She didn't know how to say, I don't want to.

"What are you going to do? Are you going to get married? Are you going to—what—just have, like, two kids or something?"

"I don't know, Brita, I don't know any of these things."

"I don't want you holding my baby anymore," Brita said softly.

"Brita—" They were both talking quietly, so as not to bother Nick.

"Just leave me alone," she said.

"Brita, don't say that."

"You already have Tiina and you already have Simon, and you can't start taking the little kids, you can't take anyone else, you can't have Anni, too."

"It doesn't work like that—"

"It does work like that. There are sides, Julia."

"No—"

"And don't you ever, ever think you are doing that to my boys. They are always, always—" she said, her voice breaking.

"I'm your sister," Julia said, but Brita just walked into the living room and sat down at the leather couch.

\* \* \*

It was Christmas before Julia faced the prospect of going home again. Not going at Thanksgiving had been as retaliatory as she could be. She'd spent it with Will, in total and utter misery. His family had gone to the movies on Thanksgiving—to the movies!—and they'd served fake whipped cream and there were decorations in the house, turkey candleholders. His siblings were uninterested in her presence. They seemed to anticipate that she wouldn't be around for long. She knew they were right. Three times she'd been sure she would never see him again and each time she'd run into him somewhere, a bar, a party, and then there was the pressure of his hand on the small of her back. There was his air of indifference against a sudden interest in her. It was nearly Christmas, and she was figuring out what kind of gift you gave to someone to prove you didn't love him, when Simon called to tell her that Christopher had been hit by a drunk driver. Not wearing his seat belt, he had been flung from the window. For a few days he lingered, paralyzed, then died.

The funeral was out in Boston, and she said he didn't have to come but Will said he would come. She could feel the obligation she put on him, but she took it, and sitting next to him on the Chinatown bus, his hand in hers, she was happy to look like a couple to outside eyes, to have this excuse to make them a real couple at last. At the church, Simon sat in the front row, holding hands with Christopher's mother. He shook so hard Julia wondered if he should be given something, some kind of medication. Her parents had not come. Brita had not come. The little girls had not come. Nels had come at the last minute, though, flying in from Minneapolis. He wore a suit and looked strangely adult. He had left his wife and kids at home.

"Everyone," Julia said, "this is Will," and he shook hands with Tiina and Nels and looked like a model boyfriend. When he sat down at the pew, he held his tie to his chest; during the service, he squeezed her hand. The minister, some cheesy, springy fellow, talked about Christopher and his love of design—Christopher had just started a position at a firm that specialized in luxury penthouses—and with every specific mention of something Christopher had done Simon heaved, and Julia, overcome with more emotions than she could catalog, began to cry and, encouraged by her own tears, cried more. When Christopher's parents went up to talk about how much they had loved Christopher, and how much he had taught them to change, she began finally to cry in earnest, crying about Christopher, and for Simon, and about Will, and for herself.

"Simon," Nels said, after the service was over. It was funny to see them together, the two brothers who had never behaved fully like brothers, who had always been so overrun by a family led by and filled with women. "I'm sorry."

Simon fell apart again, leaning over the closed casket until Nels and Will helped him stand. Watching Will at the front of the church, she thought about marrying him. But that would never happen. And if she ever married anyone, she knew, it couldn't be in a church. It would have to be like Tiina's—outdoors, a Hindu ceremony even though her husband was also not Hindu, each tradition entirely invented and lacking in gravitas and therefore not traditional at all; therefore nothing like a wedding at all. And it wasn't like they couldn't see the divorce coming—he, too, had not shown up for the funeral. Thinking about this nearly made Julia cry again.

After it was all over—the burial, the good-byes to Christopher's family, who they had only just met—they went to Simon's apartment, where Tiina said damn it all she was downing a bottle of wine, even if Nels was there, and Nels looked away. Simon sat on the couch, pressing his suit jacket to his eyes. Julia cried more, because she couldn't stand to see Simon cry, and then Tiina cried. Will looked a little tired of it all, and this made her cry harder.

Three glasses later Tiina said she hated their parents for not coming. "I can't fucking believe it," she said. "I always expected more of them. I always thought they'd rise above their own bullshit."

"Did you ever tell them that?" Will asked drily.

"We don't talk about that stuff with them." She looked at Will dismissively.

"You can't expect people to change if you never ask them to," Will said. He shrugged.

"Don't be wise," Julia said. She was drunk and at the point where the only good idea seemed to be to get more drunk. She hated Will at that moment, Will and his aphorisms and his ease. "Fine," she said, "I'm going to tell them. I'm going to tell them they can't treat Simon like this." She felt delirious.

"Everyone calm down," Nels said.

Will looked mildly entertained by the unfolding scene.

"Call," Tiina said, "call them." Simon lay nearly asleep now, on the couch.

Julia found her phone and called and, to her surprise, someone picked up, right away, her mother.

"Why aren't you guys here?" Julia said.

"Is everything okay? Honey?"

"Why aren't you here? Why do you have to be such sanctimonious assholes?" Her voice was tired from crying, and the insult came out in a dramatic, rent fashion.

"I'm hanging up."

"Six years," Julia said, shouting, "how much longer did they have to be together for you to take them seriously? When would it count?"

"We love Simon," her mother said simply, "of course we were so sorry to hear about his loss."

"Your loss," Julia said.

"It is never my job to make you feel comfortable about your lifestyle choices," her mother said. "We're here to remind you of what is right. We know you know in your hearts what the right thing is, of course we know you know that—"

"Assholes!" Julia screamed. She hung up and they sat around, exhausted.

"What a shit show," Will said. He rubbed at his eyes. "Where's Nels?"

Julia got up and looked around. "Shit," she said, "he's gone," and she ran out of the apartment, down the stairs, tripping. She didn't have her shoes on. She didn't have her coat on. She didn't see him. She stood and let people walking by stare at her as she rubbed at her arms.

She went upstairs. Will was carrying Simon to bed. Together they took off his shoes and gave him a pillow. His shirt and pants were still on, and he looked as if he, too, were suddenly dead.

Julia sat on the edge of the bed. She petted at his hair, fine and blond and stuck by sweat or tears to his head. It's o-kay, she tried to sing, it's o-kay, it's o-kay, my ba-by.

# RUPTURE

B RITA WAITED. SHE knew if she turned her head she could watch the ultrasound, see the baby flex his legs and move his arms, but she kept her eyes on the ceiling. As a rule she dealt with pregnancy by not dealing with it at all. She never looked at her belly, never admired her profile in a mirror. This late in the game you could almost see the baby through the scar, Jimmy said, but she never checked. At least Dr. Schwartz was gentle, spreading the gel slowly on her stomach, and he knew to get things over with quickly. Over coffee she always recommended him to other church moms—she liked the sheepish jut of his teeth, the way he removed his glove before he helped her sit up from the exam table.

"Well?" she said. She knew she was blushing, but she willed herself to seem calm, in control. People always thought they were brainwashed—and, worse, irresponsible—so it was important to seem like she'd always understood what she was getting into. Don't you know they invented something to fix that? the neighbor lady had said to her. Even going to the pediatrician was humiliating. Nod so I know you understand, the doctor had said, like Brita was a child. But Dr. Schwartz always behaved as if having as many children as God gave wasn't worth questioning. It was why she went back to him for all six of the boys' births, even though they had moved and it was a long drive now.

At the sink he washed his hands, and his wrists and his forearms.

"Brita," he said, "we've known each other a long time." She rearranged the folds of her gown. "The other day—" He paused. "I looked it up. The world record for C-sections is eleven. In a way that makes me feel better, but still, seven . . . it makes me nervous." He turned back to her, drying his hands one finger at a time. "We'll do another amnio next week, and with any luck we can push it early. In the meantime, do as little as possible. No housework."

"Well, I have to teach," she said.

"Teach?"

"Piano lessons. Sitting down, of course."

"I didn't know you did piano," he said.

"For years," she said, which wasn't strictly true. Two Christmases ago a neighbor had come by from next door with cookies and Brita had been balancing pennies on Paulie's wrist at the keyboard, and within six months she'd been teaching half the neighborhood kids.

"You wouldn't want to teach Jenna, would you?" he said. "We've got this nice piano but no one plays it—and she just sits on the computer all day. I've been meaning to for a while. You know." Brita tried to sit up straight and look professional, but in the gown it was impossible.

All night she wanted to tell Jimmy about the teaching but she had to do prayers alone, standing at the door to the boys' room with her hands folded over her belly, listening to their Finnish, showing them how to soften their consonants and accent the first syllable. *Isän, Pojan, ja Pyhän Hengen nimeen,* they said in turn. Through the window Brita could see the moon, high and slim in the sky. Always she felt as if Jimmy would hear the prayers and come home—when she was little her mother would say, "Dad will smell the spaghetti and come home," and sometimes Dad did—but Jimmy didn't come. When he finally made it into the bedroom and showered he still smelled of paint beneath the soap, the industrial-citrus combination she had smelled even on their wedding night, a brassy cleanness.

On her side, her hip killing her as it always did this late in the pregnancy, she said, "Dr. Schwartz wants me to teach his daughter."

"Yeah?" he said. He got into bed. He rolled up behind her, put a hand beneath her loose T-shirt. She could feel his hand avoiding the scar, moving near it but never touching it. "Who's going to watch them when you're gone?"

"My mom has to be here anyway until this is all over."

He sighed. "Honey, I'm really tired."

"I've done prayers alone four nights now," she said, feeling the frustration well suddenly.

"Honey," he said, "I'm really, really tired," his voice drifting some, and sure enough, there was the sudden small shudder of his limbs as he fell into sleep. She got up, walked around. She took her belly in her hands, held it like a bowl. She shook it, to make the baby wake, but even he slept, and she went downstairs and sat in the living room, on the fraying couch. She put her feet out and reached for the small kiddie blanket on the floor, and finally she slept, waking to the boys prodding at her face.

"Go pour cereal," she said.

Jimmy walked in, dressed already. "Did you have to?" he said.

He took his cap off, put it back on, nestled it onto his head. The sight of him, his physical self, always surprised her—how did he still look so young? Here she was with the swing of fat on her arms and her thighs getting swollen, it was all so typical and all the more sad for being typical. It was his greatest kindness, never saying his disappointment aloud.

Pull it together, she said to herself, and she sat up, and for the rest of the week she did keep it together, which she achieved largely by doing very little. She ordered pizzas they couldn't afford and watched the boys break the sprayer on the hose for the third time, and pretended not to see when they peed in the neighbor's koi pond. She called her sisters, bored, but no one picked up until Julia. In the background Brita could hear the sounds of a restaurant.

"We're out to lunch," Julia said.

"Hi, Brita!" Tiina called from the background.

"Feeling pretty big?" Julia asked.

"Yeah," Brita said, but she suddenly didn't feel like talking about it.

On Saturday finally she got ready to go to Dr. Schwartz's house, and she drove the van, its bumper hanging like a fat lip. She had planned to park on the street, but when she found Dr. Schwartz's house she realized there was nowhere to hide—his house occupied the top of a man-made hill that loomed over the street and seemed to edge over even the lake. It was a new construction but made to look older, with a columned porch and a cobblestone path. Standing on the porch she could make out the hang of saucepans over the kitchen island, and even the spray of a backyard fountain. She pushed the doorbell, and after a long while a very thin girl with a serious face came down the stairs. She looked like she hadn't washed her hair, and her eyes were rimmed with thick but neat eyeliner. She seemed somehow older than thirteen, so steadfastly did she ignore Brita's belly.

Dr. Schwartz appeared, all warmth, doing the introductions, and Brita couldn't stare at the house like she wanted to. She wanted to turn her head up to look at the spines of a chandelier in the two-story foyer, and she wanted to touch the stalks of some exotic grass that rose from a glazed pot. Instead she removed her sandals and padded after him, the tiles strangely dry under her bare feet.

In the library, Dr. Schwartz pulled a black sheet off the top of the piano, folding it. The piano was a Steinway grand, in full glisten, its legs unnicked, its belly free of fingerprints. "What a beautiful piano you have," she couldn't help saying.

"Please," Dr. Schwartz said, opening the keyboard. Jenna fiddled with her phone.

Brita sat down on the bench. She wanted only to sit for hours and play, to run through every piece she had ever known, but instead she tried out a few opening chords, a modest adagio.

"Really nice," Dr. Schwartz said, shaking his head. "What is that?"

"Beethoven," she answered. She marveled at someone who owned a piano like this but didn't know a thing like that. It was easy to forget that people who owned nice things didn't necessarily do anything with them. It made her sad to think of it, the song as old as it was in her, going back to when her father used to play late at night on the old piano, the one with the missing hammers, and upstairs the notes would sound steadily into their sleep.

"Can you play anything at all?" Brita asked Jenna, when Dr. Schwartz had left them alone.

Jenna sat on her hands. "No," she said.

"Well, do you play anything in school, did they teach you recorder, keyboard—"

"Listen," Jenna said, "it's okay, we don't have to do this." She gave a wry smile. "It's been a year since my mom, well, she left him, whatever—anyway, he's trying to be nice, so I'm trying to be nice about him being nice."

"Sure," Brita said. "Okay."

Brita played patient, tried to teach Jenna a basic scale, but Jenna wanted to learn songs her friends recognized, songs Brita didn't know, and she didn't care to keep her wrists flat and her fingers curved because, she shrugged, she could hit the notes anyway.

I already have so much character, she'd wanted to say, and she felt that was doubly true now. She wanted to be vain, she wanted a nice van, she wanted to just have life be easy, to have a big and beautiful grand that announced you weren't struggling, to have something that did no one any necessary good.

When the half hour had passed, Brita felt more nervous than when she'd arrived. She tried to slip through the kitchen with a wave.

"Well?" he said brightly. "So great to hear you playing."

"Sorry, Dad," Jenna said. "I don't think it's for me."

"Of course it is."

"Dad, be chill," Jenna said.

"What do I owe you?" he asked, turning to Brita.

"Oh," she said, "nothing, nothing, please," and she walked outside to the van, praying he would not come and wave goodbye from the porch and see her crawl into the van, but of course he did, of course he watched her pull herself up by the wheel.

"You be careful now," he called from the porch. He seemed

apologetic, even from the distance. She was closing the door when a pop can fell out onto his driveway. She debated getting out, crouching down to get it, but instead she left it, knowing he was watching her drive away. The character-building van, they had called it when she was little—it was that mortifying to drive, even then—and now, somehow, it was still running, and theirs now, a gift, if you could call it that, from her parents. I already have so much character, she'd wanted to say, and she felt that was doubly true now. She wanted to be vain, she wanted a nice van, she wanted to just have life be easy, to have a big and beautiful grand that announced you weren't struggling, to have something that did no one any tangible or necessary good.

Driving, Brita stared out at the homes along the lake, watching the mansions become homes, the homes become ranch houses, until she reached the section of town that started near the skiing range, which everyone knew was really a landfill. When she came into the house she was hit by the impoverished furniture. She stood in the middle of the floor and gave the living room her most critical look, accounting for each item: the black couch she'd sewn new covers for, covers that she had to redye twice a year, covers that she stapled shut before company came over; the rug she had convinced Jimmy to buy and which he regretted aloud once a week; the plywood floor she'd painted matte gold. On the whole the impression was of a neat, minimalist Scandinavian home, but to her everything smacked of resale, things she'd tried to refurbish but that were newly falling apart again, that would always be falling apart again.

"How was it?" Jimmy called from the kitchen. He was making something to eat; she could smell butter.

In the backyard the boys were naked. Clearly the neighbor was going to complain again. "Jimmy, the boys," she said. "*Poi-jat!*" she yelled from the back door. "Boys!" Their little white penises dangled about the yard as they ran. She sat on a chair and still she did not cry.


A check for fifty dollars came in the mail from Dr. Schwartz. "Just cash it," Jimmy said.

"It was a trial lesson," she said, "and I feel like—I feel like it's a consolation prize," she said. She kept seeing the pop can roll into his yard.

"What's that your mom is always saying?" Jimmy said. " 'Your own pride stinks.' "

"Well," she said, "pride is something to have."

"Can't afford it," he said, and he took the check and put it in his wallet. She hated that, sharing a checking account, that he could sign checks for her.

The rest of the day seemed to slip by—she went to the hospital. The needle went into her abdomen, into her uterus. She watched the fluid enter the syringe and she felt like her brain or her heart was being emptied of something. "I guess you've done this before," the tech said.

"You have no idea," Brita said. She went home. The boys begged for money to walk to the gas station, and she gave it to them. It was early the next morning when Dr. Schwartz called.

"Lungs look okay." He sounded like he hadn't slept. "We're moving it early."

"Okay," she said. "Are you sure?"

"Brita," he said, "I live in terror your uterus will just rupture on its own. To be frank."

Her mother came over. Jimmy called people at work, trying to find someone to cover for him, trying not to sound annoyed. She said good-bye to the boys. They were bored and wanted something to do. She told them only boring people were bored.

"I don't like this," she said in the van. She bit her lip and looked out the window. She remembered about the check, about the shame of cashing the check. There were too many shames.

"Honey," he said, "it's gonna be okay. Hey," he said, "don't look that way. Hey, what can I do for you? What do you want?"

"Fifty dollars. AC. A diamond ring."

"Okay," he said. "First thing. Soon as we get this done with."

"We," she said, but she kept her voice light.

In the hospital room Brita sat and waited alone. Jimmy was in the cafeteria, grabbing a bite to eat. "Before the fun starts up," he'd said. Dr. Schwartz came in, twice, but he only said that he had extra nurses to help, and that she should sit back and relax. It's not an airplane ride, she wanted to say, but she supposed that was what people said when they knew they held someone's life in their hands. She didn't like this, the feeling of helplessness. She liked to bring the van in when it broke down and make endless rounds of oatmeal baths when the boys got chicken pox, but this—there was only time to be passed. She could only let this thing happen, the C-section, the neat, circumscribed phrase that suggested nothing happening at all.

More people came in, all in scrubs, all hovering near her without speaking to her—someone put the cover on her hair, lowered her bed so she began to fall flat, and her legs were lifted, readjusted, then a cold gel on her belly, spread quickly and thickly.

Around her she could feel the room grow full with people. Nurses with weekend plans lorded them over those with more shifts. To her right she heard Dr. Schwartz talking to someone, no, to Jimmy, and she noticed that an actual clump of dirt had fallen from Jimmy's boots. He was dressed in his jeans and a neon-green T-shirt. Soon he was in the starchy green too, masked even, but his same boots still said *car-pen-ter, car-pen-ter* as he walked, his callused hands on her hair, his permanent citrus scent swallowing the smell of sterility.

"Remember when I asked you to marry me," he said. He was trying to be cute.

"I'm just going to lie here and rest," she said. She closed her eyes to Jimmy, to the sea green of nurses about her.

"Okay," he said. She heard the scraping of a chair as he pulled closer to the bed. He took her hand in his but held it as if she were a child, fingers not threaded but palms clasped. She pretended to sleep, but of course she did remember when he asked her to marry him. They'd been shopping at the mall. He'd been eating his lunch at the food court—tacos—and suddenly he couldn't feel his left side, couldn't chew, couldn't smile. The doctors at the hospital thought it was something in his brain, a stroke. He'd looked so boyish, like he needed her. Marry me, he'd said, in his hospital gown. Later they found out it was a hole in his heart; they'd sewn it up in a minute.

She turned her cheek to the side, away from Jimmy. She did not let herself cry. What should she dream about. She realized she had run out of fantasies—out of husbands to imagine, homes to build, pianos—there was nothing, only life itself, only long and hard and always more of it, always more. She forced herself to open her eyes and she studied the medical equipment, its complications—she liked complicated things, complicated machines—and craning her neck she saw the end of a cart, bags of blood hanging like deflated lungs, collapsed balloons, and their readiness paralyzed her.

Suddenly it was very quiet but for the beeping and the clatter of tools on the tray. She felt a pinching in her chest. They were doing things to her now, she knew—she remembered this, the feeling of being made of many numbed parts.

"Hold this," Dr. Schwartz kept saying. Other people talked,

but she couldn't distinguish their individual sounds, like listening to a foreign language and not knowing where words began and ended.

Again and again she heard the sound of tools against a tray, metal to metal, the hush of people listening and watching. She didn't want to look at the ceiling, or at Jimmy. A nurse came to peek at her over the curtain, and she warded her off with a smile.

"Pressure, pressure," Dr. Schwartz kept saying, his voice tight. The suction's hiss. "Tuck your hand under," Dr. Schwartz said.

She turned to watch Jimmy, to study his handsomeness, at its best in profile, his face sturdy like fresh cedar, a catalog face. Jimmy had stood up and was leaning over the curtain. "Is he out yet?" she asked. Jimmy kept watching, did not turn back to her. "I said, Is he out yet?" she repeated and she heard three or four people talk on top of one another, voices suddenly high, and someone said, "We've got a hemorrhage here," in that absurd medical calm, and then Dr. Schwartz, "Get the husband out of here." Brita thought she would throw up, hearing that she would be alone.

Jimmy said that he would stay with her. "I'm staying here," he said, and she had a brief moment of pride, gratefulness for his masculinity, for her provider and protector, but Jimmy was urged out of the room, and she wanted to call out something to him, she had a phrase in her mind, I love you, maybe. She felt heady, she felt— At the door Jimmy was red-faced to a nurse, and the cart of balloons was gone. Still the beeping carried on, the room wearing thin now, and she could make out no particular person. The image came to her of her abdomen as prey, ants to jelly on the counter, jelly on the knife, and she thought about Abraham and Isaac, about Abraham tying Isaac to the table, and she wondered how long it took him, and did he tie Isaac carefully. She thought she would try to get up, but she couldn't, she was bound, or her muscles were, and she said, or thought she said, I don't want to die, as if to ask God Himself to hold the scalpel. She noticed there was a new beep, an octave higher, doubled but not lined with the old, a syncopated shrill drumming, and she forced her chin to her chest, and she saw, caught up in the cotton, blood, her blood, steeping up from the bottom of the curtain.

For four days and three nights Brita drifted through the coma, waking on the fourth night in a bed of morphine, into a wavering world, with the sensation of an alarm missed, an accidental nakedness, nightmares she could not recall but whose presence felt permanently tattooed in her unconsciousness; even through the happiness and through the tears of others, of strangers, nurses, she felt a heaviness, like an unclean conscience—sometimes she would try to smile, but she could not. For instance, the nurses had come to her room with paper party hats that they strapped to their heads and hers, and a cake, and they all stood around her and clapped, she who should not have lived, and Jimmy was there, too, Jimmy happiest of all, if happiest was the word, and even then, even with Lars in her lap (she could not nurse him—the trauma had dried her milk) she couldn't manage the faintest smile.

"I read to you," Jimmy said. "Your favorite psalm," he said. "Did you hear me?" She tried to imagine this, Jimmy reading to her, For they that carried us away captive required of us a song, for they that wasted us required of us mirth, saying, Sing us one of the songs of Zion.

"How shall we sing the Lord's song in a strange land," she said.

"Yeah," he said.

"No," she said, "I didn't hear you."

He handed her a picture the hospital had taken of Lars. "I showed this to you," he said. "Could you see it?"

"No," she said.

Her mother and father came to see her. Other church mothers came to see her. Her sisters came to see her, Leena and Paula and Anni and Uppu. Tiina and Julia and Simon and Nels called. Her phone would not stop ringing. Everyone had the same things to say, everyone was full of the same gratitude she did not have, and their gratitude rankled her. Four times Dr. Schwartz came to see her and each time she only listened to him talk; she wouldn't, couldn't talk back. He chatted faster than before, more nervously—he gave uplifting predictions of her recovery, he introduced her to groups of interns and nurses as the "miracle mother," always shaking his head. Brita couldn't stand that he seemed sincere about his wonder, that the birth and the coma had to be a big deal; she only wanted to fast-forward to the moment where everything was casual again, a moment when she didn't have to think each minute about the fact that she had almost died—it was all so humiliating in retrospect, the shame stuck to her as she wheeled her IV into the bathroom, as the boys clambered on her bed, pushing the buttons, making it rise and fall.

I almost left them without a mother, she thought, looking at them, but instead of feeling more tenderly for them she could only despise herself. She felt insane. Or, rather, she felt as if she must have been insane before and had woken from the coma with a new brain, one that could think things through, one that gaped at the woman who had let herself be pregnant again, who hadn't had the nerve to sneak the birth control pills

Dr. Schwartz always offered. When she fed Lars his bottles she did not want to think the worst question of them all, but the question was all she could think—was he worth it?—and each time she thought it, she hated herself a little more for thinking it.

She still had water legs when Jimmy dropped off the boys for a couple hours while he ran errands. "Couldn't you find them nicer clothes?" she said to Jimmy. The boys were in T-shirts they normally wore to bed. There was an actual hole in Paulie's shirt.

The boys were bored with the hospital, they said, because it was too much like church. They had to sit still and not touch anything. They couldn't wrestle, and of course they couldn't turn on the TV. They played Communion. Paulie fed Alex and Nick and Jacob the remains of her hospital food, a spoonful of applesauce, a sip of juice.

Dr. Schwartz came in, Jenna behind him. Jenna waved, awkwardly. Brita felt too tired to manage the situation.

"They're playing church," she said, in explanation.

"Jesus says come, for all is ready," Paulie said. The boys doubled up, laughing.

"*Poijat*," she said, "*hiljaa. Nyt.*" She sat up and tried to swing her legs over the bed, but they felt like someone else's legs. She was sure stones had been sewn into her seams.

"Do you need help?" Jenna asked. The question made Brita's eyes smart. An absurd question with such an obvious answer. "I'm fine," she said. "I'm fine, really," she said, again and again, she didn't know how many times. She moved her feet to the floor. Somehow she stood. Somehow she walked to Lars, feeling like her gown was opening in back. At the very least they could see her legs, the heavy, useless stubs. She got to Lars, but she couldn't pick him up. "Paulie," she said, "pick him up."

She turned back to Dr. Schwartz, to Jenna. She saw suddenly the resemblance between them, in the manner they wore their faces, in constant worry.

In two weeks she was allowed to go home. Jimmy insisted on making a production of it, bringing her balloons and promising that the freezer was filled with lasagnas and tuna casseroles, collecting her cards and flowers into bags that he carried almost proudly out to the van, which—he pointed out twice—had AC that worked now.

Too soon there was the sight of their house, and she seemed to see this anew, and newly terrible: a small ranch, the brick painted white, the bushes thin and failing in front, the driveway's cement splintered with weeds, toys strewn under the trees. She stepped slowly to the front door, hand to sore stomach, her own mother on the porch, her quiet suggesting she was impressed by what her daughter had endured that she had not. Be gentle, her mother said, when the boys tried to hug her. They couldn't be gentle though, they hardly knew how—already they tired her, already they were so needy. Look, look, they said. Paulie stood holding the door open for her, pacing as he held it. "Mom," he said, "come on," and she made her way up the steps, more slowly than she needed to, proving to Jimmy how fragile she still was. She was fully inside the foyer when she realized she was looking at a grand piano, Dr. Schwartz's grand piano. Her hand moved to her mouth, to her chest. Everyone was watching her face, and she felt herself form what she thought was a smile, what was trying to be a smile, and she heard herself say, I can't believe it, or something of the kind.

"Dr. Schwartz had it delivered yesterday," Jimmy said. He shrugged over the boys' heads, to tell her he didn't pay for it. "Technically," he said, "it was his daughter's idea."

She turned to the piano and sat at the bench, slowly. She felt a wave of bitterness—the piano was much, much too large for the room. Its grandness was inappropriate, next to the couch with its tearing cushion, the coffee table's crack. Jenna, sending her a piano. She wanted to sit Jenna beneath the piano and have it collapse on her.

"Well, go on, play," Jimmy said.

Brita lifted the cover of the keys. Inside they lay clean and clammy. She looked up, and she saw the sun running off the top of the piano, and as if still in the morphine world she saw not a piano but a table, herself flat upon its back, wanting to get up and never able, the rest of her life stretching across its planes. Always there would be more to give, always it would be she who would have to give, and she had nothing left to give at all. For her there would only be the pittance of others' pity. That poor mother, they would all say. You poor mother, the piano said.

"Mom, play something," Paulie said, and he bent his knees up and down.

Obediently she touched her fingers to the keys, the reflection of her fingers shaking. She pushed a key so slowly it made no sound at all.

## JONAS CHAN

H E WAS THE new kid, but already he knew who Uppu
Rovaniemi was. Everyone knew who every Rovaniemi was,
the way people recited the litany of their names, the way teachers would say, "Well, we can't all be Rovaniemis," laugh, laugh.
And Uppu, as the last of the nine, inheritor of the legacy, seemed
determined to surpass them all—her impatience with stupid
people, the way she leaned in over the test and circled undoubtedly correct answers faster than he could read the questions.
And it would have always been like that, his eyes tottering after
her down the halls, except that she had sat by him in calculus
and locked her arm in his and said—knowing perfectly well he
couldn't disagree—that they ought to be friends.

Before Uppu, he'd come home and submit his backpack to
its inevitable inspection, do his math (first in pencil, then in pen),
turn down the after-school snack. "He's too anxious to eat," his
mom had reported one night at dinner.

"He's going to give himself ulcers," his dad had said.

"I have gum in my purse. You want it? You can share it," his mom said, already standing, rustling through her purse. "Make new friends."

"It's good for stomach acid, too," his dad said.

He'd tried the gum, he'd even sat next to strangers at lunch, but after he'd talked about how it never really got hot or cold in the Bay Area, and after he'd asked whether he really did need snow boots (actually, his mom had already bought him some), he would pretend to be finishing homework, to cover the quiet. The truth was that he wasn't nerdy enough for the nerds, no one cared that he came from California, and there were exactly enough Asians for him to be different without being interesting, and those Asians were Korean, and he was Chinese from Malaysia, and anyway the Koreans all went to the same church, and at lunch they held hands and prayed together. The only thing he had going for him was the viola. But who wanted to be friends because you were a good violist?

Uppu did. "Such a relief," she gushed, "to not wince when the violas come in. But you play like a violinist," she said. "Not enough weight on the bow."

"My parents made me switch," he said. He pushed at his glasses nervously.

"I knew it," she said. "I could see it a mile away. Okay. Other guesses. You practice every day. True or false."

"True," he said.

"I forgive you," she said.

She announced that they were skipping school to go to the zoo. She said it was more educational. They walked through the glass tunnel with the polar bears and held their hands up to the enormity of its paws. He stood just behind her so he could stare at a small freckle behind her ear. "His fur is getting moldy," she said. "Look, it's, like, oxidizing." Around them moms tried to push strollers and kids screamed, and the bear lolled in the water. The bear flexed its mouth in boredom.

"This is so much better than the Hutch," she said.

His dad grounded him for skipping school. He announced this via a Post-it on Jonas's door.

"Who does that?" Uppu said, when he called to tell her he was grounded. "Tell them to read some parenting books, I mean, really." She had a point; he just spent the time on the phone with her. Hours on the phone. Right now, he could hear her eating Cheetos. Her plan, she said, was to eat Cheetos and drink Mountain Dew and read science fiction all night.

"How come you aren't in trouble?" he asked.

"Oh," she said, "it's the only good thing about big families. My parents never check up on anything. Except faith." She made an ungraceful, snorting sound. "Nothing else matters," she intoned, in imitation of someone.

"How come you never talk about it?" he said. "Your church."

"It's just that insanity is so dull. Nothing to say."

"But what kind of Christianity is it, even?"

"Well," Uppu said. She stopped to eat a few Cheetos. "It's called Laestadianism. It's a kind of Lutheranism where everyone is much more hung up on being Lutheran than all the other normal Lutherans. End of story."

But really he wanted to hear her talk about it. At school he asked his stand partner. The Rovaniemis, Andy told him, were more or less brainwashed; the Rovaniemis had a million kids because they did not use birth control; the Rovaniemis did not go to school dances; the Rovaniemis did not have a TV. Andy bit fretfully at his cuticle and went back to his drawing of a ribosome he had taped to the stand. Suddenly he turned to Jonas. "Why?" he said.

"Just curious," Jonas said. This was what he told himself, anyway; after all, his parents were technically Christian, and he'd been baptized, but even in Los Gatos they had really only gone to church on holidays, and now that they'd moved, they had quit altogether. But he was also dimly aware that he was curious because he wanted to know—had to know—if the rumors were true, if the crazy church stuff meant he was never, ever going to be with Uppu.

He called his friend Billy in California. The conversation lasted six minutes. "Just go to her church," Billy said. "You can find out what it's like and she'll think it's nice of you—you'll seem really . . . gentlemanly." Billy was learning guitar and in the background there was the sound of him picking out chords. "So," Billy said, "is it snowing there yet?"

Jonas told him it wasn't.

The website said services started at eleven, and he showed up five minutes early. When he pulled open the sanctuary doors, the room was nearly empty and a little chilly. He sat toward the back. The church filled suddenly a few minutes after eleven, a couple making their way over toward his bench. They looked to be in their early twenties, and the husband carried a car seat with his arm slack, like it was heavy. Three kids trailed in front of them.

The church, he saw now, was entirely white, and moreover, everyone looked so similar it might have been a family reunion.

Uppu herself showed up after the organ had started playing, lagging behind her sisters slightly, plucking at the back of her tights. When she saw him he smiled, but she blushed and looked quickly away. She sat with her sisters in the back and folded her arms, her crossed leg beating out a nervous rhythm.

When the sermon began he realized almost immediately that the minister must be her father. She had his face, especially his eyes. He felt hurt she hadn't told him about this. He tried to listen, but he felt too distracted—once one baby cried they all cried, like dogs—and the heavy woman in front of him kept reaching into her purse and taking out a single marshmallow. She chewed the marshmallow like gum. Then, carefully, she selected the next marshmallow. And Uppu's father spoke very slowly, to his hands, or to the windows. There was much mention of forgiveness, much talk of just being human—"God understands," her father said, "how often and easily we fail"— and on the whole it didn't seem particularly strange. Unlike his family's old church, no one said they loved Jesus, no one was overemotional, and God was less a personal friend than someone spoken of quietly, as if in fear of disturbing Him. Afterward, people came up to him, asked where he was from, how he knew Uppu. They said it was great he was thinking of music school. Someone invited him to come again next week.

At school, Uppu reamed him. She spent three days not speaking to him at all, and after he had written her note upon note that she returned, she finally broke down in the parking lot and told him that she was humiliated and that now everyone thought they were going out and her parents had lectured her about not dating school boys and it looked like she had invited him and everything about it was insane and he could never come again.

"Ever," she said, "ever."

"Fine," he said, cowed. "It's just church, okay."

"You don't understand," she said. "You didn't grow up with this, I grew up with this. It's not just church, it's not just anything. I love," she said, "that you have nothing to do with it. Don't ruin it, Jonas, please, please." And then she kissed him.

And with that his life became her car, that dear cheap crappy car, with heat and AC that only worked at the highest setting, and a driver's seat stuck permanently a little too far from the pedals for Uppu's legs, so she shoved a large teddy bear behind her back. And even when he was kissing her, when he was trying to pull her from the driver's seat, the teddy bear was always there, or they pulled it over the gear shift so that her thigh would not jam into it when they were undressing in a fervor. But they did not have sex. They did not talk about sex, but both bodies agreed not to do it.

One night she picked him up and they drove out to where the suburbs dwindled into houses with actual acreage—an actual horse chewing beside the car, its jaw moving side to side, side to side—and as they began their feverish clamberings he tried not to but still he saw the littered candy wrappers on the floor, he saw sweaters, he saw a crumpled catechism even, he saw rolling and emptied cans of pop. He had nearly forgotten about these things when her phone rang in the cup holder. "Where are you?" he heard her father ask her, tinny, distant. Uppu broke several laws on the ride home through the small backcountry roads. They were going to hit a deer, but they didn't hit a deer. She dropped him off and, as she later reported to him, she arrived home to find her father on the porch, pacing.

"Where's Jonas," he said.

Uppu told the only lie she could tell. They had been discussing faith matters.

His world pulled and refracted with a mighty tug.

\* \* \*

The dog, a small, bug-eyed thing, wriggled in Uppu's arms, but she kept it pinned to her chest. "So when you say you're interested in the church, do you mean you're going out to coffee with my daughter or that you're having casual sex?" her father asked.

"Um," Jonas said. He cleared his throat.

Her father looked mostly out the window behind Jonas.

"Can you take that thing out," her father said softly, and Uppu put the dog out on the chain in the backyard but immediately it began to bark.

The table was an old, soft wood and Jonas found that if he pressed hard enough into it with his thumbnail he could leave a permanent ridge.

The conversation took two hours. Uppu sat through the whole thing, unwilling, uneasy. She was a different being: silent, almost statuesque. Uppu's mother, with the name he couldn't say aloud, Pirjo, darted in and out of the kitchen, refilling her coffee. Jonas listened diligently to slow commentary on the church and modesty and vanity and forgiveness—how converting just meant asking forgiveness, nothing else. All you had to do was ask your sins forgiven, her father said, looking at his hands. That was all. Then you were a believer. You were in the church. Once you had the heart of a believer, he said, the restrictions weren't restrictions at all—it was simply what your conscience told you to do and not do. There wasn't a rule at all about no TV, but their consciences told them it would be better to stay away from that kind of temptation.

"It's really," her dad said, "the simplest thing in the world. It's a simple faith."

"See," Uppu said after.

"See what," Jonas said.

"The madness."

"At least they do what they say. Practice what they preach."

"Some," she said, "not all." She smiled her mischievous smile.

He started going to church, in part to uphold Uppu's lie but also because it was a way to spend time with Uppu. Immediately he began to see her parents relax some, and when he came over they were even nice, almost intensely so. It was his birthday and her mother baked him a cake and hung balloons from the chandelier. In the dining room they lowered the lights and the table was surrounded with them, with Brita and her boys, with Uppu, her parents, Paula, Anni—everyone on pitch, in harmony, singing first in English, then in Finnish. "It doesn't exactly translate," Pirjo explained. "We aren't really saying happy birthday, we're saying, joy, lots of joy to you." They gave him presents they had made: a mail holder from a clementine box, pie weights made from pennies, a scarf. They sat around the table and played board games until his eyes hurt, Uppu dancing around the table when she won. "Sheepie queen," she chanted, "sheepie queen," and her dad rolled his eyes and ate ice cream from the box.

His mother was almost desperate to have Uppu over for dinner. "Can't we meet your new friend?" she said. When he came home from school she was planning the menu, stir-fried vegetables, tofu with black bean sauce, a whole steamed fish with tomato and garlic sauce—"Does she like garlic?"—and he said it was all fine, everything was fine, but at the last minute she baked a frozen pizza, too, the smell of its burning crust filtering up to his room.

Uppu came with a braid of Finnish bread she had baked herself. She told them her favorite classes were physics and math. She admired the piano, a modest upright, and, when asked, played them a Debussy nocturne, fudging the middle a little, shrugging her shoulders as she played through it to the end, to a final chord that fell easily into place.

"Why can't you be more like your friend here," his dad said. Jonas wondered if Uppu could understand their accents.

"Both piano and violin!" his mother said. "You must practice all the time."

"Ha," Jonas said.

"Well, I'm really not very disciplined," she said. She had taken small servings of everything, and ate slowly, with little bites.

"You're just being modest," his mom said.

"No, really," she said.

"Jonas only has to practice on the days he eats," his dad said. "That's what his old teacher used to say."

"Jonas has really great technique," Uppu said. "He's going to get into a top conservatory." She wiped at her mouth with the corner of the cloth napkin.

His dad laughed, but it came out like a single, heavy breath.

On the phone later Uppu said his parents were awful to him. "How do you do that?" she said. "Is that supposed to be modesty or something?"

"They just expect a lot from me," he said.

"Still!" she said. "Are they ever nice to you?"

"Of course they're nice to me," he said, and it was true. They were nice in that they gave all their time for him—everything was for him, his dad's new job at Ford, which was more money for a better viola teacher, for the test prep classes, his mom's constant care, always remembering his exam dates better than he did. But he didn't want to tell her this—it wouldn't fit her definition of nice—and he didn't want to tell her the other things, how his mom slept in the master bedroom and his dad slept in the guest room, how he had heard his dad once saying that he wished they'd had more than one child. How it was only rarely now his dad made his mom laugh; it used to be all the time, and when she laughed he could see why they were together, his dad's jokes taking away his mom's anxieties. Now his father drank more, and that made his mother worry more.

But they had both admired Uppu. She was good with them in the same way she was good with teachers, suddenly deferential and careful and talking with adult distance of college or the war or the problem with the lack of a truly mainstream media. His parents suggested that she come over again. When he did his math homework they wondered if he should call her for help. And even when he went to more and more church activities with her, they let it go. He would come back from church and they would ask how it was, and he would say fine, not freeing them of their impression that it was a normal church.

"Should we come with you?" his mom asked. He hated this, how she was always trying to be supportive, so eager to show him she cared, when really, he thought, she just didn't have enough to worry about. In Los Gatos she had never fussed about whether doorknobs were polished, whether they had run out of extra meat in the extra freezer.

"He'll pray for us heathens—they have to," his dad said.

"Well, maybe we'll come for Christmas," his mom said.

"Maybe," he said, but already he knew he would find an excuse. He couldn't have said why, but the idea of them at Uppu's church was preposterous.


At church he began singing along with the hymns—those strangely minor melodies, like songs of mourning—but quietly, as if disinterested. Uppu always sang, simply, stolidly, like singing was a task that had to be done and must be made the best of. He had been coming to church all winter now, and he recognized everyone, or, at least, they all recognized him. He knew the Jankkilas, and the Hillukas, and that they were cousins, and that you could tell them apart by their chins. He met the woman who ate marshmallows during church.

"So where are you from?" she asked.

"Same suburb as the Rovaniemis," he said, "just north of the mall?"

"No, before that," she said, and finally he realized she just wanted to know that he was Chinese from Malaysia, so he said that.

"You speak very good English," she said.

"They live in their own little world," Uppu said in the car. "Sorry that always happens to you."

"It's just Peggy," he said.

"No," she said, "Peggy just says what everyone else thinks. It's the fat lady's job."

She always talked like this, as if everyone at church was an idiot, but then again it was the same tack she took with people at school. She said he could stop coming to church any day now, but he said he didn't really mind. He started actually listening to the sermons. Uppu suggested he ignore them but he found this very difficult, especially if her dad began to cry. And sometimes her father seemed to be speaking straight to him— not that he ever made eye contact with him, but Jonas began to have an uncomfortable feeling that all the bits about unbelief were directed at him, and all the bits about the sins of the flesh. That phrase, the sins of the flesh, began to follow him like a specter—the entire phrase was so humiliating, so revolting, that for it to be associated with him seemed unimaginable, and a few days after hearing a sermon about selling your faith cheaply for the lusts of the world he found himself trying to reclasp Uppu's bra, which was difficult, much more difficult than undoing it in the first place. Her skin took on a broil, like she had been hit.

"Sorry," he said, "it just—it feels weird."

She pulled on her sweater and turned her back to him. "Uppu?" he said. He reached out for her.

"You don't want to touch me, don't touch me," she said. Her ears were a perfectly bright red.

He tried to hug her, but she didn't move. He held her like that for a long time, until she reached out and took hold of his hand.

Now when they hung out they abided by a new and unspoken code—they retreated into an earlier stage, where they kissed carefully and slowly and then stopped, Uppu sometimes pushing at the rules; maybe, he sensed, trying to tease him beyond them. She had a way, for instance, of running her finger along the band of his boxers, or unbuttoning his jeans, and then suddenly stopping, as if he had told her to stop, as if to say, That's where your overboard conscience gets you.

One night song services were at her parents' house. "You don't have to come," she said, but he went. Like every Sunday, it was strange to see her how the church saw her—her hair hanging simply, her clothing modest, her socks clean and matched, polite, shaking hands, slicing cucumbers, setting out the nice spoons, the nice coffee china.

In the quiet between songs, he suggested a hymn. He could feel Uppu looking at him. He could feel her parents' small smiles.

"What was that all about," Uppu said afterward. She said it like she was teasing, but she wasn't.

"It's just a song," he said.

"Okay," she said skeptically. Later, when he was talking to someone, she stood very close behind him, like they were a couple. While he stood there she put her hand on his lower back. He felt the trace of her thumb along his spine. When he leaned back into her hand, she took it away.

Undoubtedly everything between them was weird now. In only a few months Uppu was, quote unquote, being dragged over her dead and dying body to a church college in Finland for a year, and he'd be at Michigan, and because he could not bear to acknowledge this future and because Uppu said she was trying to store up positive memories to get her through the sunless land, they did not talk of it. At school they behaved relatively the same—for so long they had maintained an outer facade of platonic friendship that they kept easily to it—but now when they disappeared at lunch out to her car he could tell she was equally unsure what to do. She seemed edgy. Usually she stole things from the lunch his mom had packed him, but now she just ate her apple and unrolled the window and threw the core at someone's For Sale sign. She had good aim.

"Is everything okay?" he said.

"Sure."

"I mean, what's going on with us?" he asked.

"We're just not, you know," she said.

"You're okay?" he ventured. He ate the rice from his rice compartment.

"You know," she said, "some days I think it's incredible I haven't left it yet, and some days it's like I know in my deepest place that I can never leave it, that I'll always come back, that this is just a phase, I just think I'm so cool right now and one day I'll wake up and realize what an idiot I am. So I think ultimately, maybe, my problem is just that I'm too self-aware, like I get my own future too much, I get how dumb I'm being right now." She said this all very quickly, as if it was something she had been thinking for too long.

"Yeah," he said.

"I'm such a coward," she said sadly. She took his lunch bag, began rifling through it.

With only a week left of school—the air warming so that he could smell, he thought, dirt—she drove them off campus during lunch.

"Um," he said, "can I ask where we're going?"

"America's Roller Coast," she said. She smiled at him. She squeezed his hand.

It took two hours to get there, and once they were there she refused to follow the person waving a red flag. She cut in line, and she insisted on riding only the same huge coasters, again and again, and on one ride she looked at him just as he was sure he was about to vomit, but seeing her eyes on him sustained him through the moment. When they finally left it was dark—his feet hurt, he had a sunburn along his hairline. They scouted out the car. She didn't put her seat belt on, just sat with the keys in her lap.

"Jonas," she said. She turned and looked at him, and as always, he couldn't fully meet her eyes, and he looked at the sun setting behind the skeletons of the coasters.

She climbed out of her seat and undid his seat belt and made room for herself next to him. She put her head on his shoulder. "Don't let me go."

"Uppu," he said, and he readjusted his body, put his arm around her. She felt pliable, and she smelled of sun and sweat. He kissed her forehead, he kissed the top of her nose, he kissed her mouth, they kissed. He pulled at her pants, and she pulled at them with him, and then they pulled at his, hurriedly. The lot around them was emptying, the sky was nearly dark, there was the distant sound of people yelling about rides, about where their cars were. Someone had to find a bathroom. He pushed those things away, he thought only of Uppu. He questioned nothing, what they were doing, or why, or where they were, or why she had a condom in her purse.

When the sex was over she lay over him like a child in a parent's arms, their shirts still on. Finally she climbed over to the driver's seat. She got dressed and unrolled the window. He didn't know what to do with the used condom. He found a yellow napkin in the glove box and wrapped it in the napkin like something dead. He put his clothing on, quickly.

"Well," she said, as they pulled away, as they got back on the highway.

"Yeah," he said.

When the car hit eighty she took the napkin he'd been holding and let it slip out the window. She took his hand.


The night of his graduation party it rained, and the celebrators huddled under the tent his parents had set up, and ran from the tent to the open back door, or stood in the garage and looked at his father's gardening tools hung along the walls. His aunt and uncle had flown in from California, and a few neighbors had come, and his stand partner, and his viola teacher, but there were just the ten of them or so, until the Rovaniemis showed up; Brita came, and all her boys, and Leena and her toddler, and Paula and Anni, and Pirjo and Warren, and Uppu, and soon where there had been ten people there were at least twenty, plus whining kids, all trying to fit into the garage and under the food tent, and his mother was frantically frying more shrimp in the kitchen, running back and forth with an umbrella, carrying aluminum foil pans of shrimp and calamari that the Rovaniemis looked at before picking out a few of the miniature cakes. Uppu stood next to the food with his father, talking about what, he didn't know—probably making studying in Finland seem like a great opportunity, and tonight his dad would say, You should study abroad like Uppu.

Pirjo came up to shake his hand. She handed him a new Bible. Inside, someone had written, To Jonas, with hope.

"We'll keep seeing you around, I hope," she said.

"Sure, I mean, I'll only be a half an hour away." Behind her he could see Uppu, his father laughing at something she'd said, the way he never laughed anymore. He was getting drunk, too, and he set his hand by accident into a bowl of rice and his fingers came up covered in bits of white grains and Uppu laughed and he laughed.

"At church, I mean," Pirjo said. He felt mortified, like there was some larger thing that was required of him but, being so immature, he was unable to do it.

She hugged him. His mother came by, carrying a six-pack of beer. He wished she wasn't doing that, he wanted to tell her not to do that.

"You must be so proud of Jonas," Pirjo said, her arm still around his shoulders.

"He tries," his mother said.

The Rovaniemis left and their relatives went home and they left behind a backyard of quiet that no one could fill again. He felt it again, the largeness of them, at Uppu's graduation, though then the entire church showed, every room filled, even the stairs, even the porch, forty or fifty little kids running about, a few babies lying on blankets atop the living room rug, waving their limbs like beetles on their backs. There was no beer. Paula was in the kitchen, her hair pulled back in a tight bun, racing trays back and forth. At some point Pirjo rounded everyone up and made them sing. She insisted that Uppu pick her favorite song and Uppu reluctantly did, the one with dramatic words, the fiery hearts quenched by blood, the seas of love.

Jonas watched her sing with everyone, her eyebrows furrowed and earnest for a minute.

Uppu's nephews were clinging to his knees—Jonas taught them how to draw a tank—when Pirjo came to him with more cake and pulla.

"She'll be gone in a week," Pirjo said.

"Yeah," he said.

"She'll be back before you know it, though," she said. He blushed at this implication. Thinking about blushing made him blush more. "Well," she said, sipping her coffee, "while there's life, there's hope."

"Mrs. Rovaniemi—"

"Pirjo."

"No," he said, "but—" For strength he took a bite of cake.

"Tank," the little boy said, and tugged at his pants.

"In a minute," Pirjo said, and she shooed him away. "Yes?" she said, to him again. She looked at him intently.

"I'm—"

"Well?" she said.

"I don't know. I feel—" He searched for how he felt; at the moment he felt anxious about Uppu. "I don't feel great," he said. He crumpled a napkin in his hand, suddenly saw Uppu unrolling the car window, the napkin flying out of her fingers. "Things," he said, "things I've done."

"Oh, Jonas," she said. She didn't reach out to touch him. "I know," she said. "I know. We're just human, we make mistakes. That's why we're so lucky—" She frowned hard to stop her tears, and her face was suddenly ugly. She wiped at an eye. "Jonas," she said, her voice quiet but certain, "would you like to have the sin of unbelief forgiven?"

He looked down at his cake.

"Sure," he said, and she hugged him, and he tried to hang on to the cake behind her back as she said, in his ear, the words, the absolution, so familiar now but still so strange—in Jesus's name and blood. As she hugged him he felt her small shoulders shaking, like holding a frog cupped in his hand, and then he began to cry, too, crying through a lifetime of never being good enough and a lifetime of not being loved enough and the kindness of her, and the want of Uppu, and the want of this life, and he cried because now it seemed he might have it. Everything, he realized, could be had now.

Pirjo let go of him and stood back, handed him a napkin—it was blue and white, for Finland—and they both blew their noses, and laughed a little.

Uppu's father appeared, eyebrows raised.

"Jonas has just received the grace of repentance," Pirjo said quietly, and Warren said, "I'm so glad to hear that." He shook Jonas's hand. "God's Peace, Jonas," he said.

Uppu came by, Leena's toddler on her hip like he wasn't a toddler. "What's going on here," she said. Jonas wiped his glasses, put them back on.

"Jonas has just received the grace of repentance," Pirjo said.

Uppu looked like she was going to laugh. "What," she said again. "Really?" She looked at him. She looked for something in his face.

"Yes," he said. He felt himself smiling, trying not to smile, smiling.

"Okay," she said. She nodded. "Okay." She turned around, and she began to walk, in her slow, calm Uppu way that meant she was the most dangerous—it reminded him of when she had told him, for instance, that you always walked, you never ran, when you were about to leave a store with something stolen in your pocket—and she went to the top of the piano, where all of the graduation cards were. She began taking out the money, the tens, the occasional twenties. She took the checks. He walked up to her.

"Hey," he said.

"Please leave me alone," she said quietly. He put his hand on her arm. She removed his hand from her arm.

He left her alone. In the dining room people came up to him and more people shook his hand. Everyone was very bright and very happy and Peggy Maki hugged him so that he felt how huge her breasts were—massive—but he kept listening for the sound of Uppu.

By the time everyone was leaving no one could find her. "She'll show," Pirjo said, "she's probably outside with someone."

He called her, ten times, twelve times, but she didn't pick up. Finally he left, he drove home, he climbed into bed, his happiness mixed with terror. Part of him felt like he would sleep like a baby, and part of him feared he would never sleep again—he could not believe he had joined the church, he could believe he had joined the church. He was a believer. He could marry Uppu. Except Uppu was mad at him—but he remembered what she had said to him, in the car, that she would always come back, that she always did.

The next morning was Sunday and his mom brought him the house phone. It felt solid and clunky in his hand.

"Jonas," Pirjo said, "God's Peace."

"God's Peace," he said, feeling like he was in a play, saying a part he didn't know.

"Sorry to bother you. I found your number in the phone book."

"It's okay," he said.

"Uppu isn't there, is she?"

"No, why?"

"Warren," she said, "she's not with Jonas." She hung up.

At church he sat next to Pirjo and Warren. It turned out that Uppu was still gone. Her car was gone. But they were calm—she was a little headstrong but she always came home, and where could she go? Why would she go? This was Pirjo's reasoning. Anyway you had to wait twenty-four hours to report anyone as missing, and besides, she was eighteen.

He spent the day at the Rovaniemis', at their kitchen table, eating the leftovers from the party, running load after load in the dishwasher.

"They are the best of me, you know," Pirjo said to him. "They are the best thing I ever did with my life, my nine." Her face looked moist but it might have been the steam from the dishwasher. Each time the phone rang they all went for it, but Pirjo always won. Around dinner, at last, Uppu's sister called, Tiina, the unbeliever, in New York. Uppu had driven through the night without stopping to Tiina and Perry's place on the Upper West Side and now Tiina had given her two sleeping pills. Uppu was not coming home. Uppu was not going to the church college. Tiina would try to make her call later.

"Well," Pirjo said. She put her hand on Jonas's arm. "I know this is hard."

He went home. He tried calling Uppu even though he knew it was no use. He left her a message each time, the same message, I love you. Please come home. It was all he knew to say. She didn't call.

The next Sunday he sat with Pirjo and Warren, but Pirjo bowed her head the whole time, and Warren asked the congregation to pray for Uppu, his voice choking, his forehead nearly touching the pulpit, and the Sunday after that Jonas sat in the back row near the troubled youths, who used pocketknives to drill holes into the backs of the pews, and for two years he stayed there next to the troubled youths, in the rightmost corner. When Beth Kariniemi began to talk to him too much after church, inviting him to play viola with her in the Christmas program, he began arriving late and leaving early, and each time before he opened the sanctuary doors he would think—she is going to be there, she is going to be there—but every week she was not, and every week he was full of a great grief, but every week he came back, and every week he was forgiven.

## WHISKEY DRAGON, 1847

N O ONE WANTED to marry her. For years she had gone to Easter church, watching every last one of her enemies and then every last one of her friends walk proudly to the altar in their brightest clothes. She had eaten their meat, drunk their whiskey, but no man appeared at her family's tent, his reindeer dressed in bells. After what had happened to her father, she was bad luck. Her family was bad luck. There had never been any other child but her, and she was plain, and then she had become old, and for many years it had been just her and her mother, their tent always farthest on the edge of the siida. But now Aslak had appeared to ask her to marry him— homely, crude Aslak, yes—and her hands shook with an intensity of joy.

Her mother did not want her to do it. His family were famous drunks—his brother came to services with a bottle in his hand and mocked the priest from the back pew—and Aslak was reputed to be just as heavy a drinker, if quieter about it. But life had already shown her that there were worse things than whiskey, and so she had come outside to greet him. He was wearing his whitest furs, and she unharnessed his reindeer and took him into the tent, where they sat in silence for some time with her mother's coffee.

She was disappointed that her wedding morning felt so ordinary. Laestadius was marrying them, with his heavy dark hair and brow, with his dramatic airs. She had expected him to be grander about the service, the way he was when he gave his sermons, storming about at the altar, causing women to cry and roll their eyes, making girls faint from visions. But he was dressed in typical settler black, and his family sat watching on the bench, also in black, his wife Brita nodding and somber. Behind them very few had come to witness the wedding—there were some patches of red and blue caps, and an old woman who rocked back and forth. Laestadius kept his voice low, the sermon quiet. "Remember, dear ones," he said, "the evil that threatens you even now on your wedding day, that threatens your children, that threatens us all." He stopped abruptly, and his voice grew sterner, tighter. "The time of the whiskey dragon is at its end," he called out. "You are murdering your children," he said, "with every drop you drink," and Gunnà wished he would talk about love.

Finally he made them recite the words—Aslak had to try several times, for he was already a little drunk—and all in all it had felt like any other spring Sunday, even the eating and drinking. She had wanted things to feel different, she had wanted to be a different Gunnà, recognized by all as something of a prize, but she knew, watching the whiskey dribble down his hairless chin, watching him wipe at the dribble with the back of his hand, that they were nothing but a foolish pair, Gunnà and Aslak, the bad-luck charm and the no-good drunk, her rough, wide face and his chapped cheeks. Even his hand in hers felt clumsy, and when they went outside after the ceremony to exchange reindeer she saw that her choices were fine and white and his were stunted, with short legs. But she would not let herself be disappointed in him; she would not let herself begin, so soon, to define the grievances of a lifetime.

They passed the spring in her family's siida. At night her mother came to visit and Gunnà cooked her coffee and they listened to the men working, the sound of their axes against the hard crusts of snow, the sound of the reindeer shuffling behind them as they lipped at the uncovered moss.

Spring was always a hard season, because they had to prepare for the migration north to the sea, and it was harder now with Aslak's herd, too—their herds were not used to mixing together, and they balked at the presence of the additional bulls. The worst was that Aslak did drink heavily, it was true. When he drank he came home and reached for her in a way that she knew was meant to be affectionate but made her nervous, how he became desperate, pawing off her clothes. It was an ugly side of him, and she didn't want to see it.

But sometimes he went into the church-village and did not come home at all. Her mother would come visit her in the tent. She would say nothing, just sew small things—boots, mittens, things for the baby Gunnà was not pregnant with— and click her tongue. The dogs would crawl into the tent with her—they followed her mother everywhere, because she gave them bits of fat—and Gunnà would sit and hope desperately for the sound of Aslak's sledge outside, but then night would come and she would sleep alone under the furs. In the morning she would emerge to find that he was not yet there, and she would go out herself to watch the herd, returning to the tents at night to find the barkeep and Aslak in the corral,

Aslak putting his knife into the throat of a young male reindeer, the reindeer stumbling for too long before it finally stopped. Gunnà balked at the shame, of a husband who could not kill a reindeer quickly, of a husband who drank so much it cost an entire head.

Her mother shook her head sadly. "You should take him to church," she said. "I heard that's what Inger did, but then all of those Maggas are even worse."

Gunnà said nothing. She worried that her mother would mention Laestadius in front of Aslak again. He hated him—he hadn't even wanted to be married at the church, but these days there was no other way to do it.

"Laestadius himself is a drunk," Aslak always said. He insisted on all the old ways, all the old superstitions, always pouring out a bit of his coffee or whiskey for the earth-Haldes, reciting the Lord's Prayer in three tongues when he spied a wolf track. He said someone in his family had once been a shaman, a few generations ago, but Gunnà did not believe this.

At night she asked him, softly, if he could stay with her at the tents, and not take the sledge into the church-village anymore. It was very costly, she said.

He said nothing. He was carving something—it was one thing he was good at, and he would carve some supple, small deer but then throw it straight into the fire.

"I'm the one who watches the herd," he said. "Sometimes all night."

"But," she said, though she was not sure it was entirely true, "I need you here, for what's coming."

He kept carving, but she saw on his face that he was surprised. That night when they lay down to sleep he put his nose on the back of her neck, and she felt its cold tip. She did not smell whiskey, only him and the hay of the waning fire.

*   *   *

It took them three weeks to move the herds north to the sea, but the travel was easy, and Gunnà discovered that her suspicions were right—she would give birth in late autumn. When they reached the sea the days had lightened fully, and even in the tent sunlight seeped through at night, and she covered her eyes with the furs to sleep, but she was anxious with happiness—it crept up in her throat and kept her from sleeping. She would awake, brimming with fullness, and pace outside, watching the reindeer curled up like dogs in the distance on the fells, some of the calves awake, idle.

She loved the reindeer that summer, even the loud rush of lowing all the calves made at once, even the frantic pace of marking the calves, the men with their lassos, the herd running in its endless circle away from the singing ropes, the calves crying as the marks were cut into their ears. At night Aslak went out to fish and in the evening they sat in the summer light of night and beat mosquitoes from each other's backs and ate sweet, sharp berries.

Even her mother, always moody near the sea—never liking to remember her father's drowning—was cheerful. She was cheerful about Gunnà's baby, and she was kinder to Aslak, going to extra lengths to sew his things or dry a new pelt.

Once even Gunnà walked late at night with Aslak, her hand in his. They walked to a turn in the cape, where they could see out across the sea, where large plains of ice still sat, frozen, drifting on the water.

"It was like this," she said. She recalled, evenly, the sight of her father far off on the floe with the hundreds of heads of reindeer, where they had run to escape the mosquitoes, and where her father had gone to chase them back, before the ice had given way. She had been just a small girl and her mother had keened, shrieking as the reindeer had struggled, the tessellation of their antlers briefly visible above the water, her father's hat visible for a moment, but they were so far out to sea, so small, and it had looked like a dream, almost a beautiful dream, the sea suddenly still as if nothing had been called under.

Aslak took her hand. Things now, she felt, were different—that was the luck of the past. She wasn't even sure if she believed in things like luck, and she decided she would not worry; she decided, staring out to the sea, that from now on everything was different, and she turned to look at their herd, in the distance, eating calmly on the fells, safe, safe.

They delayed the migration south for three days, and then they could delay it no longer. Around them the other herders had already set off, the sound of their bells long gone. Aslak worried, though, that the walking would make the baby come.

"She won't be the first woman to have a baby on the walk," her mother said, but Aslak sent her to the back of the herd, where she would be able to rest when the reindeer rested, instead of leading the strings with the draft reindeer, which carried all of their clothes and slaughtered meat and tents.

They had hardly crossed the third river on the fourth day when she felt the first straining of muscle inside her. She took the stick she was carrying and beat at the reindeer closest to her, to pass on her pain to something else, anything else. Near her Aslak's cousins urged the herd on, the dogs biting at their ankles. She called to the nearest boy, and he came and helped her set up a small tent near an outcropping of rock. He found a dog and tied the dog to a tree. She lay beneath the tent and he gathered food, and skins, and water.

By the time the baby was born she felt she understood those

who wandered out into the tundra and let the cold kill them. Around her the hay was full of her blood and feces and the thick liquids of afterbirth. She was proud that she did not want to vomit. She had always been like that, fearless when she was supposed to cook the reindeers' brains, or ladle their blood into the pots. "Let me do it," she would say when her father went to slaughter the bulls. He let her watch. "I don't know how you do that," her mother would say. "You're nothing like me." Now, though, her mother cut the cord with her knife and washed the baby in snow she had carried down from higher on the mountain. How small the baby was, how red, how angry. Gunnà was wild with pain, she felt delusional from the pain, and she wiped desperately at herself with snow, and her mother gave the baby a bit of reindeer fat to suck on, and Gunnà tucked the baby in her tunic, against her skin, to quiet her.

For two days they sat and she rested. Her mother washed the baby three times a day in the snow, and she pampered Gunnà, mixing her sour milk and herbs, giving her the softest furs to lie on. But they could not wait, and on the third day Gunnà stood and they packed the small tent and began the walk. As they walked Gunnà sang. *Voia, voia, voia, nana, nana, nana*, my poor witless husband, she sang, *voia, voia, voia, nana, nana, nana*, what will become of us, when will we reach the reindeer, when will come the end of this suffering?

She grew sick. Every movement hurt, and she was so tired she could hardly eat. Her mother fed her, but she threw up the meat and drank only small cups of milk. She heard them talk of sending for the highlands shaman, whom everyone knew had raised the drowned boy from the dead—but the most important thing, she knew, more important than her, than the baby, was to get the herd to the wintering place, before the days grew completely sunless and they had to travel in the dark. She worried ceaselessly over the baby, though she could see that it was healthier than she was. The baby hung in the pack off the lead reindeer, only her eyes showing out amid fur, but still Gunnà worried. Once a sparrow had nearly landed on the hood of the cradle and she had gone mad, trying to beat it away. When they stopped to rest her mother brought her the cradle and she opened her tunic and let the baby feed, though her breasts froze and felt numb.

"Listen," Aslak said at night, "do you think you can walk yet?" Every day he asked. Every day she rose to show him and nearly fell.

"It's something in the blood," his cousin said, and they bled her, but she felt worse than before.

Aslak sat at night in the tent, his forehead furrowed. "Aren't I worth it?" she said to him, her voice low so her mother would not hear. She put her nose to his nose.

"Ah," he said tiredly. He sighed. She ladled him the coffee her mother had cooked, but he did not drink it. He took out a bottle and gave it a long sip.

"Aslak," she said.

"How's Little-Bell," he asked. It was her name for the child, because she made so much noise with her babbling that it reminded Gunnà of the smallest reindeer's bells. Her mother looked at Little-Bell, asleep in the cradle.

"She eats," her mother said. "At least one of them eats."

He stood up and left.

"When winter comes," her mother said, "you must watch him. He will drink away the herd." Gunnà listened for the sound of his steps outside but he was already gone.

\* \* \*

By the time they reached the wintering place, the reindeer were already too thin. They were worn, from working too hard to get at the moss along the way, and they had lost several calves in the river crossing, and three to a wolf, despite the dogs setting upon the wolf, the snarls of which Gunnà could hear even from her sledge at the front of the string, even across the tundra full of their hundreds of heads of reindeer.

"There are no good omens," her mother said. "I don't like it."

Aslak thought her mother's talking was a bad omen. He was moody now, and never in the tent, always coming in long after the dark had fallen, his cheeks cracked from the cold, so that Gunnà rubbed and rubbed reindeer fat onto his face but still his cheeks bled in places.

"Did you sew today?" he said. The skins had rotted in the damp of the migration, and there was much that had to be done, before the true cold of winter set in and their hands would be too stiff for the work.

"Ha," her mother said.

"Soon," Gunnà said. It was true she did not yet feel herself, but also true that she could have done much more now. Her mother was always the one with Little-Bell, dangling beads in her face so she laughed, so the Uldas would not come and replace Little-Bell with one of their own ugly children. For herself she was afraid to spend too much time with Little-Bell, afraid that her illness would spread somehow, and anyway her mother handled the baby so much more capably.

At night she smelled Aslak behind her, the stink of his sweaty skins, the stink of whiskey.

"Why?" she said.

"It keeps me warm," he said, "it keeps me awake. So the wolves don't—so the wolves don't make me sleepy," he said. He smiled at the tale, she could hear it as he talked.

"No," she said, "I'm not ready yet." She could not bear the thought of her body being touched again, of her body being used again. It still hurt to walk, and to sit, and especially sitting in the sledge was painful, the way it bumped over the hardened snow.

"Gunnà," he said, and he nuzzled behind her.

"I'm resting," she said.

"You're always resting."

Her mother hissed, from across the tent.

He rose and sat in front of the fire, laying the wood carefully.

She pretended to sleep, but she watched him drink. He drank it like it did not hurt his throat. He sucked at the bottle. He poured some of the whiskey onto the ground, muttering, and she knew it was a prayer to the earth-Haldes. The fire grew very hot, so she could feel the frost on the inside of the tent turn to fog. Her cheeks grew moist with the fog. Next to her, Little-Bell stirred, whined, and she sat rolled over to feed her. Her breasts hurt, but at least in the warm fire it was not so bad as before. She felt Aslak's eyes on her as she fed Little-Bell.

"*Voia, voia, voia, nana, nana, nana,*" he sang, "there is my beloved, there is my fox fire, *voia, voia, voia*—" He stopped suddenly. He drank more. "*Nana, nana, nana,*" he started again, "who says there is love, who says there is this thing . . ."

She lay back down and pulled the skins tight around herself, tucking Little-Bell in next to her. The fire was down to cinders when she felt Aslak crawl in beside Little-Bell, and felt his hand cross over Little-Bell to her stomach, felt his hand finally relax into sleep.

*  *  *

When she woke Little-Bell was not moving. Little-Bell was not breathing. Her eyes sat back in her head like a dead reindeer on the trail.

"Aslak," she screamed, "Aslak!"

She shook him violently. Aslak did not stir, so heavily did he sleep.

She screamed again. She shook Little-Bell again.

Her mother rose finally, and came over, and began to scream, and Aslak awoke. He saw the baby—her head was turned horribly to one side, like it was broken. Her mouth and eyes were frozen open.

Her mother screamed and screamed. Gunnà screamed. "Little-Bell," she said. She bent over her. She ran out for snow, and brought it back, and rubbed it on her, like she did for frostbite. She kneaded it again, and again, onto Little-Bell's face, onto her arms. "Little-Bell," she said. Her tears fell onto Little-Bell's face, onto the small tunic her mother had so neatly sewn for her, and her tears began hardening into ice. From the other tents Aslak's cousins came running, their boots not yet stuffed with hay. They looked in—What is it, they said, what is it, but Gunnà could not bring herself to say. She looked at Aslak, his bleary eyes, his heavy body. She did not want to think what might have been true, what it might have been that had killed Little-Bell, the heavy, drunken weight, the unfeeling mass of her own husband.

Aslak sang to her. Her mother sang to her, about a child who drowned in the sea. For many days she did not move, and the dogs sat at her feet and did not move, at Aslak's command.

They licked her exposed ankle. Still she did not speak. She lay on hay spread over the skins in the tent and drank melted snow, and reindeer's milk. Sometimes she chewed on a small piece of cheese. They were supposed to have taken Little-Bell's body to a graveyard, they were supposed to carry her body with them on the sledges to the church, but she would not allow it. She made Aslak wrap the body in birch bark and leave it on an islet, beneath the whitest birch. Everything of Little-Bell's she burned. The clothing, the cradle, even the small husk of doll Aslak had made for her.

Sometimes she sat inside the door to the tent and looked out, watching Aslak come home from tending the herd. She would not sleep on the same side of the tent with Aslak anymore. She wished there was a way to keep him from the tent forever, and when he came in and she smelled whiskey she rolled over onto her side.

While he slept was the only time she went out. She took her skis and went out in the dark to the herd, where she skied around them and watched them sleep. She looked for wolves. She watched the reindeer, how simple their lives were. What did they think of? Where the moss was, how thick the snow was.

It was the darkest part of winter when they all set off for town, as they did every winter, for the church service. She did not want to go, but it was the law and they could not afford the fine. They rode in their nicest sledges, and they put bells along the reindeer, and they made the many-hour ride, the snow smoking up from the reindeers' hooves, the snow sticking to everything, even her eyelashes, so that she hardly saw it when the church-village appeared, its haven of four wooden buildings and its steeple, the clusters of church-tents set up and being set up, the other sledges drawn and tied to the trees, reindeer shaking their heads, kicking at the packed snow—but as they approached they heard men shouting, they saw women standing to the side, pushing children away and trying to steer them toward the church.

"What is it?" her mother called. "Can you see?"

When their sledges had stopped they climbed out and made their way to the crowd. A man all in black—Laestadius, she saw, who had married them—was dumping large barrels into the snow. Whiskey, she saw, she could smell it; even in the cold, it carried to her nose. At his feet and puddling down the small hill whiskey was pooling, turning the snow a deep brown, and men scattered at his feet, on their knees, eating the snow with their hands.

He lifted men from their knees, making them stand. "Are you an animal? Are you not made in the very image of God?" She looked to see what Aslak was doing. He stood, watching, sullen, not with the shouting men or the quiet women, just watching, like he did not quite get what was happening. "Animals!" the priest said, and without speaking he began to walk, briskly. When he began to move others began to move, and the men on the ground did look like animals, worse than animals.

She turned to look at Aslak. "Are you coming?" she said.

"He can go to his hell," he said.

"The fine," she said. She did not want to beg him in front of the crowd.

"He doesn't tell me what to do," he said, and the men near him patted him on the back, and she walked with her mother up the small incline to the church, with its drafty wooden walls and its hard benches, full now of the red and blue caps of women, women desperate to hear this man, who would fix their men, who might make them reindeer watchers again.

They were singing already, and there was nowhere to sit—it was full—and at first she stood in the back, but her legs were tired and so she made her way up the side, her head down so no one could look at her too long, and she sat in the front row and a woman in black made room for her. When she sat down she realized it was his wife, Brita—she realized the children were his children. Their faces were all so narrow, and they watched their father with admiration.

Laestadius was speaking, Laestadius was raving. She felt it, the anger. She felt the way he called at her, was saddened at her and at Aslak. She was not saved. She had not accepted Jesus Christ as her savior. She had not asked and called upon the man on the cross to save her from all she had done. It was her own sins that had led her to such a life, her own sins that had let her choose such a husband, a husband who drank like it would save him. She had been vain and she had been hopeful and the wages of sin was death.

He recounted visiting a woman on one of his journeys, a Lapp named Maija. She came from a poor family, he said, and her stepfather had wanted her to marry an old man. Maija did not want to marry this man, and she had refused, and her stepfather beat her. He had beat her before, many times when he was drunk, but this time, she pushed him, and he fell against the fireplace. She worried what might have happened to him. She knew that those who did not honor their parents were condemned, and she worried about the devil, coming for her even then. But she determined to run away. She set off in a boat, knowing her stepfather was drunk, but still he came for her, and brought her back and promised her she would not have to marry the old man. But he lied to her. The next day they brought the old man to her. He threatened to mark her with his knife if she was not quiet, but her brother heard her scream and came for her.

So Maija fled. She did not know where to go. What is sin? Maija wondered. What is right and what is wrong? Maija found a ride in a sledge, but in talking about her worries and her sins and her hate of her stepfather's drinking, she found out the people in the sledge themselves were sinners, sinners and drinkers. They said she was a bore, and they abandoned her in the wilderness. She nearly died, but she walked, Laestadius said, and she made her way to a minister. And this minister— Laestadius was speaking quietly now—this minister taught her about her sins. He taught her that any evil in her, any sin she had ever committed, could be washed away in the blood of the Lord and Savior Jesus Christ. And from this woman, this simple Lapp, he had learned his own unrighteousness. He had been saved from his own eternity of hell. He paused for breath. He wiped some spittle from his mouth. "Believe and follow the bloody footsteps of Jesus," Laestadius said, "from the garden to the hill of Golgotha. Hasten to gather drops of atoning blood into your polluted vessels before death overtakes you!"

Around her, women rose from their seats and raised their hands. Women clutched at their necks. A whining, strangled sound swelled through the hall. Behind them a woman rose and stood on the pew. She pulled her kerchief from her head and pulled at her hair. "I confess," she cried, "I have sinned." Women reached up around her and touched her hem. "Believe," they said, nearly as one, weeping their encouragement. Brita turned to Gunnà and put a small, worn hand on Gunnà's knee.

"Do you want to be forgiven?" Brita said. "Do you confess your own unrighteousness?"

"I don't know," Gunnà said.

"Be saved," Brita said, "as he saved me." Gunnà looked at Brita, at her face, tired and smoothed as driftwood, the hair white along the temples.

"My child is dead."

"God also called one of our own," Brita said, nodding. Sudden tears sat along her eyelids but did not fall. "But you can be comforted, as I was, knowing your child has been taken into heaven." She leaned forward.

"Heaven," Gunnà said.

"The upper world," Brita said helpfully.

Gunnà thought, briefly, of the vision she had heard the shamans describe, people drifting on their stomachs through the sky, dead people floating down rivers in the sky.

"God will give again," Brita said.

"When I woke she was already dead."

"God is merciful. God hears even your prayers."

"Then He will not give me any more," Gunnà said. She rose and made her way past the grieving women and past the staring women, down the aisle and out of the church, into the cold, into the dark. She could not see the sledges, her sledge. She could barely make out the smoke rising from the church-tents, where everyone would eat tonight, where there would be more sermons and more praying and more singing, more men biding away their fury about the whiskey.

She walked down to the inn, where the whiskey had been spoiled. Inside, men sat around a table and laughed angrily. They stopped talking when she came in.

"Aslak," she said, "let's go home."

"I'm talking," he said. Somehow he was drunk.

She went back outside. She looked up at the church at the top of the hill. Through the windows she could make out the unsteady candlelight. She heard the sound then of singing, not like the wandering songs of the Lapps but like a slow, steady melody with a straight point and a clean end.

She went to their sledge and patted the thin fur on one of the reindeers' antlers. She climbed into the sledge and flicked the reins. For a moment they stirred but did not move, uncertain. She flicked at them again with the reins and they began to run, the snow kicking back into her face, onto her hands. *Voia, voia, voia*, she sang, fly fast as the sparrows. *Voia, voia, voia, nana, nana, nana*, she sang, take me to my Little-Bell, take me to her home.

# Acknowledgments

This book was written with the support of the University of Michigan MFA Program and Helen Zell, and with the invaluable counsel of Peter Ho Davies, Michael Byers, Eileen Pollack, Nicholas Delbanco, Stephanie Grant, Amy Williams, Gillian Blake, John Weinstock, Ian Pylväinen, Emily McLaughlin, and Miriam Lawrence. In addition, I am indebted to the encouragement of Mary Elise Johnson, Marin, and Sammy Sater, and to the long-suffering readership of Ilana Sichel, Esmé Weijun Wang, and Helena Pylväinen.

## ABOUT THE AUTHOR

HANNA PYLVÄINEN is from suburban Detroit. She graduated from Mount Holyoke College and received her MFA from the University of Michigan, where she was also a Postgraduate Zell Fellow. She is the recipient of residencies from the MacDowell Colony and the Headlands Center for the Arts and a fellowship at the Fine Arts Work Center in Provincetown.